"I think we should forget last night even happened."

Kelsey almost slurred the words together in her rush to get them said.

It was exactly what he'd been expecting, but Gage felt the knot in his gut cinch just a little tighter. Forget about last night? Pretend he'd never held her, never been inside her, never felt her body shudder under his? Easier to forget his own name.

"Why?"

"I think it's best," she said. "I don't want to change things between us, Gage."

Too late. Things already *had* changed. He wasn't sitting across the table from a woman who was his friend. He was sitting across the table from a woman who he'd made love to, a woman he wanted to make love to again....

Dear Reader,

Welcome to another month of fabulous reading here at Silhouette Intimate Moments. As always, we've put together six terrific books for your reading pleasure, starting with *Another Man's Wife* by Dallas Schulze. This is another of our Heartbreakers titles, as well as the latest in her miniseries entitled A Family Circle. As usual with one of this author's titles, you won't want to miss it.

Next up is *Iain Ross's Woman* by Emilie Richards. This, too, is part of a miniseries, The Men of Midnight. This is a suspenseful and deeply emotional book that I predict will end up on your "keeper" shelf.

The rest of the month is filled out with new titles by Nikki Benjamin, *The Wedding Venture;* Susan Mallery, *The Only Way Out;* Suzanne Brockmann, *Not Without Risk;* and Nancy Gideon, *For Mercy's Sake*. Every one of them provides exactly the sort of romantic excitement you've come to expect from Intimate Moments.

In months to come, look for more reading from some of the best authors in the business. We've got books coming up from Linda Turner, Judith Duncan, Naomi Horton and Paula Detmer Riggs, to name only a few. So come back next month—and every month—to Silhouette Intimate Moments, where romance is the name of the game.

Yours,
Leslie Wainger
Senior Editor and Editorial Coordinator

Please address questions and book requests to:
Silhouette Reader Service
U.S.: 3010 Walden Ave., P.O. Box 1325, Buffalo, NY 14269
Canadian: P.O. Box 609, Fort Erie, Ont. L2A 5X3

Dallas Schulze

ANOTHER MAN'S WIFE

Silhouette®
INTIMATE™ MOMENTS®

Published by Silhouette Books

America's Publisher of Contemporary Romance

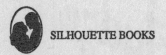 SILHOUETTE BOOKS

ISBN 0-373-07643-6

ANOTHER MAN'S WIFE

Copyright © 1995 by Dallas Schulze

This edition published by arrangement with Harlequin Enterprises B.V.

® and TM are trademarks of Harlequin Enterprises B.V., used under
license. Trademarks indicated with ® are registered in the United States
Patent and Trademark Office, the Canadian Trade Marks Office and in
other countries.

Printed in U.S.A.

Books by Dallas Schulze

Silhouette Intimate Moments

Moment to Moment #170
Donovan's Promise #247
The Vow #318
The Baby Bargain #377
Everything but Marriage #414
The Hell-Raiser #462
Secondhand Husband #500
Michael's Father #565
Snow Bride #584
*A Very Convenient Marriage #608
*Another Man's Wife #643

*A Family Circle

Silhouette Books

Birds, Bees and Babies 1994
"Cullen's Child"

DALLAS SCHULZE

loves books, old movies, her husband and her cat, not necessarily in that order. A sucker for a happy ending, her writing has given her an outlet for her imagination. Dallas hopes that readers have half as much fun with her books as she does! She has more hobbies than there is space to list them, but is currently working on a doll collection. Dallas loves to hear from her readers, and you can write to her at P.O. Box 241, Verdugo City, CA 91046.

Prologue

It was the first time he'd stood up as best man at a wedding, but Gage Walker was pretty clear on what his duties were. He was supposed to hand Rick the ring at the appropriate moment, make a toast to the newlyweds at the reception and act as escort to the maid of honor. So far, he hadn't done too badly. He hadn't dropped the ring, his speech had drawn the requisite number of chuckles and the maid of honor attached herself to her own fiancée at the earliest possible moment, relieving Gage of the responsibility of entertaining her.

So far, so good. He'd discharged his duties to his best friend, had done everything he was supposed to do. There was only one problem, one thing not working out the way it should.

The best man was not supposed to lust after the bride.

He wasn't supposed to have this gut-level urge to pull her into his arms and see if her mouth tasted as warm and lush as it looked. To slide his fingers into her hair, pull it free of the pins that held it in a soft twist at the back of her head and see it tumble over his hands like pale gold strands of silk. Gage didn't need to consult a pocket copy of Miss Manners to know that he had no business feeling the way he did when he looked at his best friend's brand-new wife.

"Rick told us that you build bridges, Gage. That sounds so exciting."

Gage dragged his gaze away from the bride and looked at the woman who'd spoken. The peach formal she wore told him that she was one of the bridesmaids, which meant that he must have been introduced to her.

"I have a little help," he said dryly, trying to remember her name. Mary or Marie, he thought. Or was this the one named Clair? They were sisters and looked too much alike for his jet-lagged brain to sort them out.

"Rick said you were flying in this morning from Austria, just for the wedding." She sighed. "I've always wanted to see Austria. All those lovely pastries. Of course, I'd have to be careful not to eat too many of them," she added, smoothing her hand over her waist in a way that drew attention to her slim figure.

At another time, Gage might have been inclined to respond to the blatant invitation in her eyes. The way she was looking at him made it clear that her hunger ran to something with fewer calories and more meat than a strudel. He had no objection to a woman making a play for him. Especially one as attractive as Clair or Mary or whoever she was. But he wasn't in the mood today.

"Actually I was in Australia, not Austria," he told her.

She laughed softly. "Geography never was my best subject."

Gage was willing to bet that she'd excelled in topics that weren't graded in most high schools. His eyes drifted past her to where Rick and his bride stood talking to an elderly couple on the other side of the room.

"Have you known Kelsey long?" he asked.

"Since high school. We met during cheerleader try-outs. I made the team and she didn't, but we became friends anyway." She glanced over her shoulder, following his gaze to the newlyweds. "They look good together, don't they? Both so fair."

Gage murmured his agreement. They *did* make a handsome couple. Rick, tall and blond, looking uncharacteristically sophisticated in his black tux, and Kelsey, her slender body curved against his, her eyes adoring as she looked up at him.

Gage looked away, telling himself that the pang he felt was indigestion. He sure as hell wasn't jealous of his best friend. Envious, maybe, of the happiness Rick had found, but not jealous.

"So you just got in this morning?" Clair—he was almost positive this one was Clair—asked.

"Late last night, actually." He reached for his champagne, considered his exhaustion and picked up his water glass instead. More than one glass of champagne in his current jet-lagged condition and he could find himself observing the rest of the reception from under the table.

"Then you didn't even get to meet Kelsey until after the wedding," Clair said.

"That's right." He'd been too concerned about handing the ring to Rick without dropping it to really look at the bride during the ceremony. It was only when they arrived at the reception and Rick introduced him to his new wife that Gage had felt the ground shift under his feet.

"It's so nice to finally meet you, Gage. Rick has told me all about you." Kelsey smiled up at him, her eyes warm and welcoming.

"Don't believe everything he says. He's always been jealous of me." Gage reached out to take the hand she offered.

At the first contact, he felt a jolt of electricity run up his arm. From the startled way her eyes jerked to his, he knew she'd felt it, too. Awareness, pure and simple. Only there was nothing simple about it at all. But Gage wasn't thinking about that in those first seconds. He was only thinking that she had the most beautiful eyes he'd ever seen in his life. Her eyes were gray. Not blue gray, but a clear, crystalline shade of gray that seemed to see right into his soul.

He had the odd sensation of destiny hovering over his shoulder, of fate grinning at him. His smile faded and his hand tightened over hers. Kelsey stared at him, hardly seeming to breathe. Time stood still.

"Did I do good or what?" Rick's voice shattered the moment.

Gage released Kelsey's hand as if it had suddenly caught fire. It had to be too many hours on a plane and too little sleep, he told himself as he responded to his friend's question with the assurance that he'd done very good indeed. Exhaustion could do funny things

*to a man's mind, even make him think of things like
fate and destiny when he met his best friend's bride of
less than an hour.*

The problem was, those thoughts stayed with him
as the reception wore on. He found himself watching
Kelsey, the way the light caught in her hair, the way her
face lit up when she smiled. And she smiled a lot. Why
shouldn't she? She was a bride, right? Brides were
supposed to be happy.

And best men were supposed to be happy that the
bride was happy. Gage took a swallow of water and let
his eyes drift to the newlyweds again. He *was* happy.
He was glad Rick had found the woman of his dreams.
That odd moment of awareness had been a momentary aberration, that's all—a combination of jet lag
and exhaustion. Hell, his body still thought he was in
Australia. It was no wonder he was hallucinating.

"Excuse me," he said to Clair, "I haven't danced
with the bride yet."

Rick and Kelsey were talking to Kelsey's parents
when Gage approached. He exchanged pleasantries
with the older couple before turning to Rick.

"Does the best man get to dance with the bride?"

"I don't know. Depends on whether or not the bride
minds having her toes stepped on." Rick looked down
at his wife, his light blue eyes laughing. "What do you
think, sweetheart? Are you willing to take a chance?"

"I think I can take the risk, considering Gage came
so far just to make sure you didn't lose the ring,"
Kelsey said lightly. But Gage saw the hint of wariness
in her eyes and knew she was thinking of that flash of
awareness that had shot between them.

"Ignore him," Gage told her, nodding at Rick. "Like I said before, he's always been jealous of me. Just because he dances like Fred Flintstone—"

"Yeah, right. And I suppose you're Fred Astaire," Rick jeered as Kelsey stepped toward Gage.

"If the top hat fits," Gage said with a grin.

Kelsey was chuckling as they walked away. But her laughter faded when the music shifted from a light rock-and-roll tune to a slow, dreamy ballad just as they reached the floor. She hesitated a moment, and Gage half expected her to say that she wanted to wait this one out, but she turned toward him, a polite smile fixed firmly in place. His own hesitation was imperceptible before he took her into his arms.

Big mistake. That was the first thought that ran through his head as he felt her slide into his arms. This was not a good idea. He felt that same jolt of electricity he'd felt before, that shock of awareness that ran over his skin, as if he'd just grabbed hold of a live wire.

They swayed to the music, the full skirt of her wedding dress brushing against his legs as they moved together. Neither of them spoke. She fit in his arms as if made to be there, Gage thought reluctantly. He tried to think of something to say to break the silence between them, something light and amusing to dissipate the tension. Unfortunately the only thing he could think of was that he wished he'd met Kelsey months ago, before she and Rick fell in love.

Don't be a jerk, he told himself. Even if he *had* met her first, there was no reason to think things would have turned out any differently. She loved Rick and he loved her. Besides, Rick was the marrying, settle-down-with-a-family type, which was more than Gage could say, or even wanted to say, about himself. He'd known for a long time that hearth-and-home wasn't for him. He didn't want—could never have—that kind of life. No white picket fences and diapers lay in his future.

"Rick and I have been friends a long time," he said, breaking the tense silence.

Kelsey tilted her head back to look up at him, her gray eyes questioning. "Since high school. He told me how close you are."

"Rick?" Gage arched one dark brow in question. "I bet he didn't put it quite that way. Not unless he was drunk at the time." He knew Rick too well to believe that he'd say anything even remotely sentimental.

Kelsey looked annoyed, caught the laughter in his blue eyes and smiled reluctantly. "He may not have phrased it *exactly* like that," she admitted primly. "But I knew what he meant."

"Yeah, Rick isn't much for pretty speeches," Gage said, grinning at the understatement. He refused to notice the soft curve of her waist beneath his hand or the light floral scent that drifted from her pale gold hair.

"Not everyone is blessed with a glib tongue, Gage." Her pointed look made it clear whom she was talking about.

He gave her a guileless smile. "Gee, thanks. I didn't think you'd noticed."

She laughed and he felt her relax in his hold. Whatever subtle tension had been between them dissipated, washed away on shared laughter. By the time Gage returned her to Rick, he'd convinced himself that the attraction he'd felt had been nothing more than temporary insanity, a momentary envy that his friend had found something he'd never risk trying for.

An hour later, when the bride and groom made their departure, Gage waved and cheered with the rest of the guests. He ignored the vague feeling of loss, telling himself it was just that Rick's marriage was bound to mean changes in their friendship.

The end of an era, he thought, pouring himself a glass of champagne. This vague melancholy had nothing to do with any fancy he might have had about destiny or fate hovering over his shoulder. And it certainly had nothing to do with how right his best friend's wife had felt in his arms.

Gage lifted the champagne flute and offered a silent toast to the newlyweds. They had their whole lives in front of them, and he wished them well.

Chapter 1

Three Years Later

Gage pulled the rental car up to the curb and shut off the engine. But he stayed where he was for a moment, staring out the windshield at the gray drizzle that was falling. Too light for rain, too heavy for mist, the omnipresent dampness seemed to cut right through clothing and chill all the way to the bone.

Confronted with low temperatures and persistent moisture, California natives commented that at least they didn't have to worry about drought this year. Tourists who'd flown west to escape snow and cold stared out their motel windows and hoped for a glimpse of the fabled sunshine, drought be damned.

Gage wasn't thinking about either the ever-present threat of drought or of ruined vacations. With a grim twinge of humor, he thought that the weather suited his mood—bleak and gray. He didn't want to be here. He wanted to be six thousand miles away, fighting off mosquitoes, flies and insects he couldn't put a name to, slogging through muck and mud, sweaty and filthy and complaining about the heat.

He'd rather be doing damned near anything than sitting in this sardine can of a car, trying not to think about what lay up that curving brick walkway, behind the closed door of the unexceptional house at its end.

Cursing his own cowardice, he shoved open the car door and levered his long legs out from behind the steering wheel. Once out, he slammed the door shut and then stood staring across the roof of the car at the house in question. It looked just the way it always did. The way it had last time he'd been here, four months ago, just before Thanksgiving.

If anything, it looked better. The lawn was brilliant green from the winter rains, and a smattering of pansies brightened the flower beds that lined the walkway. The landscaping set off the one-story structure, which was painted white with blue gray trim. It was a picture-postcard image of the American dream.

Only this particular dream had been shattered.

Gage glanced up at the sky and then looked back at the house. He didn't want to go in but he could hardly stand in the rain forever. Hunching his shoulders beneath his light denim jacket, he forced himself to walk around the car. The chill he felt had nothing to do with the weather and everything to do with the reason he was here.

Rick was dead.

Walking slowly up the pathway, he remembered the hours he and Rick had spent laying the bricks, arguing over how they should be positioned. Kelsey had sat on the lawn, holding the baby and laughing at the two of them. When Rick had picked up the hose and threatened to squirt her with it, she'd held the baby up, pretending to hide behind his tiny body. Rick had swooped down on her, wresting the laughing infant from her, and Gage had exacted revenge for the two of them by turning the hose on her, drenching her thoroughly while Rick and little Daniel laughed.

That had been just last summer. Those hot July days had been some of the best Gage could remember.

Gone. All gone. The desolate words kept rhythm with the sound of his boot heels on the porch steps. All the laughter, all the friendship, forever gone. When Rick had married Kelsey, Gage had braced himself to lose a friend. Instead, he'd gained one. Things had shifted, changed, but the three of them had created new ties. It was as if his friendship with Rick had simply widened to encompass Kelsey, as if the three of them had known each other forever. He sometimes found it hard to remember a time when Kelsey hadn't been part of his life. Rick's wife, baby Daniel's mother, his friend.

Gage closed his eyes, flickering images of half a hundred memories playing through his mind. If one of them was going to die young, it should have been him. He was the one who spent his time crawling around on I-beams, checking to make sure the bridges he'd helped to design were being put together properly. He was the one who spent ten months out of every year in parts of the world where law was sometimes more a vague concept than a solid reality.

If one of them had to die, it shouldn't have been Rick, with his nine-to-five job and his family. He'd had so much to live for. Everything had been so right in his life. Kelsey and Rick had come damned close to making him think that happy endings were a possibility.

Only fate had stepped in and proved that happy endings were the province of books and movies, not real life.

Gage realized that he'd been standing in front of the door, staring at it as if it were an alien artifact, something he'd never seen before. He didn't need help figuring out why he'd rather stand in the rain than knock on the door he'd helped Rick paint right after he and Kelsey moved in. Once Kelsey opened that door, it would all become real. There'd be no denying the truth.

Rick was dead. The reality of that lay behind that door. He'd see it in Kelsey's eyes. Rick was gone.

Gage forced himself to move forward. Rick was dead whether he knocked on that door or not. His boots sounded loud on the wooden porch. His knock sounded even louder.

He stood there, damp and chilled, trying to think of what he was going to say to Kelsey when she opened the door. He'd had the long journey from Brazil to try to come up with the right words, but they still eluded him. What did you say to your best friend's widow?

He turned away from the door to stare at one of the hanging baskets of flowers that lined the edge of the porch. Kelsey's handiwork, no doubt. According to Rick, her thumb was so green, he half expected to see the furniture sprout leaves. The baskets were certainly beautiful, he thought, concentrating on the way the solid green of leaves and the bright pinks and oranges of the flowers stood out with harsh brilliance against the drizzly gray sky behind the baskets.

He heard the door open and he turned, his shoulders braced as if for a fight.

"Gage." Kelsey's voice held no discernible emotion. And the fine mesh of the screen made it difficult to read her expression.

"Kelsey." Gage hesitated, all the carefully rehearsed phrases failing him. There simply were no words he could give her.

They stared at each other in silence for a moment. Without a word, Kelsey pushed open the screen door, and Gage stepped into the small entryway. It had to be his imagination that made the small house feel empty, as if something vital was gone from it.

"I came as soon as I could," Gage said as Kelsey shut the door behind him, closing out the dampness. He moved to put his arms around her, realized how wet his jacket was and stopped. But not before he saw Kelsey flinch as if she couldn't bear to be touched. His brows rose and he started to speak—though he didn't know what he was going to say—but she spoke before he could, suddenly becoming animated.

"You're soaked through. What did you do—walk all the way from South America?" she scolded, her voice bright and brittle. "Get that coat off before you catch pneumonia."

Gage shrugged out of his denim jacket, letting her take it from him and put it on a hanger from the coat closet.

"I'll hang this in the bathroom to dry."

"Thanks."

She'd lost weight, he thought, watching her walk away. She hadn't had it to lose. She looked fragile, breakable as a china figurine. And just about as brittle, he thought as she walked back down the hall toward him.

"How was your trip?" she asked as if there was nothing to differentiate this visit from any other he'd made. Her mouth was curved in a smile that didn't reach her eyes.

"It was fine. I'd have been here sooner but I didn't get the news about—"

"Your shirt's a little damp," Kelsey interrupted him. She reached out to pat the sleeve of his light cotton shirt as if confirming its dampness, but Gage thought there was a plea in the nervous little gesture. "Would you like something to change into?"

One of Rick's shirts?

"No!" He drew a deep breath and forced himself to repeat the word with less force. "No, thanks. I won't melt."

"I didn't think you would." She gave him another of those quick, meaningless smiles. "How about some coffee? And I baked cookies this morning—chocolate chip. One of your favorites, if I remember right."

"Kelsey—"

"There's some cake if you don't want cookies."

"I don't—"

"Or I could make you a sandwich." Her hands twisted together in front of her, her eyes shifting uneasily from his face to a point somewhere past his shoulder. "Did they feed you on the plane? Even if they did, it probably wasn't very good. You must be starving. I'll make—"

"Kelsey." Gage reached out to catch her hands, stilling their frantic movements. He ignored her compulsive move to pull away. "I'm not hungry."

"You'd probably like something hot," she said as if he hadn't spoken. "I made soup last night, and there's plenty left over. I cooked too much. You know I always cook like I'm feeding an army."

"Kelsey." Gage tightened his grip on her fingers, willing her to look at him. "I didn't fly six thousand miles to get a hot meal."

"I know." There was a pause, and then she finally lifted her eyes to his, letting him see the raw pain. When she spoke, it was in broken little half sentences, her voice nearly cracking on every word. "I know you didn't. It's just that...I'm not sure I can..." She stopped and closed her eyes. "It hurts so much," she whispered finally.

Something hard and painful twisted inside him. He released her hands and put his arms around her, drawing her against him.

"I know."

Kelsey let her head rest against Gage's chest. For the first time in over a month, she let herself lean on someone else, let his strength shore her up, emotionally as well as physically. Gage was here. She didn't have to be quite so strong anymore.

She felt hard-held walls tremble inside her, threatening to give way. She'd built those walls deliberately, needing them to hold back the pain and the fear that had nearly overwhelmed her in those first dark hours after she'd learned that Rick was gone.

Tears burned the backs of her eyes, but she forced them away. If she started crying now, she didn't know if she'd ever stop. With a sound that hovered perilously close to a sob, she drew away, forcing a shaky half smile as she looked up at him.

"I'm glad you're here."

"I'd have been here sooner, but it took a while to get word to me and then it took another week for me to get to an airport."

"I didn't know how to get hold of you, but I knew Cole would."

Cole was Gage's younger brother. He'd known Rick and Kelsey on a casual basis.

"He got a message to me but it took a while. I'm sorry I wasn't here right away." His blue eyes were dark with worry.

"There wasn't anything you could have done." Kelsey pushed a lock of pale gold hair back from her face, trying to look as if she didn't want to collapse in a sobbing heap at his feet. "There wasn't anything anyone could do," she said, shrugging a little.

"What happened? Cole's message said it was a car accident."

"Yes." Kelsey shivered a little, and Gage immediately apologized for the question.

"I shouldn't have asked," he said quickly.

"No, that's okay." Kelsey ran her fingers through her hair and sighed. "Why don't we go in the kitchen and I'll make some coffee."

"Where's Danny?" he asked as he followed her into the big kitchen.

"I put him down for a nap a few minutes ago. With luck, he'll sleep for another hour or so. You won't believe how much he's grown since Thanksgiving." For the first time, her smile was genuine. Her son was the only bright spot in her life, the only thing keeping her sane.

Gage leaned one hip against the oak counter. She felt him watching her as she got out the coffee and measured it into the filter. That was one of the things that always surprised her about him—his ability to let a silence stretch. Rick hated silences—*had* hated, she corrected herself painfully.

"How's Danny doing?"

"Better than I am." She understood that he was asking after more than his godson's physical well-being. She shrugged a little as she poured water into the coffeemaker and turned it on. "He's too young to understand what's going on. He misses R-Rick." She stumbled a little over the name but recovered and went on, her voice steady. "But it's been over a month, and that's a long time when you're not quite two. I've tried not to let him see how upset I am, tried to keep everything as normal as possible for him. I think he's doing all right."

"I'm sure he is."

"I hope so." Kelsey sighed and looked around the kitchen, feeling a little lost without something to occupy her hands. She'd discovered that if she just kept busy enough, she didn't have time to think as much. "Are you sure you don't want something to eat? I've been doing a lot of cooking lately, and there's plenty of leftovers."

Gage wasn't interested in food but he guessed that she needed something to do so he nodded. "A bowl of soup sounds great," he lied. "They fed us a dry sandwich somewhere over Omaha, but that was a long time ago."

"I'll put some on to heat." Kelsey opened the refrigerator and pulled out a square plastic container.

Gage watched her move around the kitchen, getting out a pan and pouring the soup into it. Memories teased the corners of his mind—of other times when he'd sat at the oak table that dominated one end of the big room and watched Kelsey cook; of Rick's teasing her about buying the house because of the kitchen and the fact that it sat on an acre of land. The decrepit condition of the house was the only reason they'd been able to buy it. Kelsey had been left a sizable chunk of money by her grandmother, which had enabled them to make the down payment. Should have been enough to buy a small town, Rick had groused, not one falling-down house on an acre of overgrown land.

"It's a good area. Land this close to Solvang is expensive," Kelsey told him.

"The roof leaks like a sieve, every window is cracked or broken and it looks like a family of gorillas has been living in it for the past fifteen years. But Kelsey likes the kitchen and she wants the land." Rick rolled his eyes in Gage's direction.

"Roofs and windows can be fixed," Kelsey answered serenely. *"Why do you think I married you?"*

Rick gave her an affronted look. "I thought you loved me for my mind."

"It's a perfectly nice mind," she assured him, patting his hand in a kindly way. *"But I like your strong back and ability to swing a hammer even more."*

"Do you see what a heartless woman I married?" Rick asked Gage.

"I've always admired practicality in a woman," Gage said with a grin.

"How are you at putting on roofs?" Kelsey asked, eyeing him speculatively.

Gage shook the memory away. That had been the first summer after Kelsey and Rick were married. Gage had had two months between jobs and he'd spent most of that time putting a new roof on this house.

Kelsey set the soup on the stove and then got two coffee mugs. She pulled the pot out before the coffee had finished dripping, and drops of liquid sizzled on the burner as she filled the mugs. She slid the pot back into place and then carried the mugs to the table. Gage sat down across from her, cupping his hand around the thick china, feeling the warmth of it against his palm, wishing it could drive out the chill he felt deep inside. They sat without speaking for a few minutes, only the steady drip of the coffeemaker and the almost inaudible hiss of the rain outside breaking the silence.

"Rick had gone to Los Angeles," Kelsey said abruptly as if no time had passed between his question and her answer. "He had a client there who needed to meet with him after work. He bought Rick dinner and they worked late. Rick called me around nine. He... told me not to wait up for him."

She paused to regain control of her voice. When she continued, her tone was flat, emotionless, as if she were reciting something that had happened to someone else. In an odd way she felt as if it had. She'd gone over the facts in her mind a thousand times but she could never quite connect them to Rick.

"I went to bed. It was about five o'clock in the morning when the police came. They said he was coming up the Pacific Coast Highway. It was raining. They think he might have braked for an animal that ran across the road. The car went off the road. It was in a place where there was a drop to the beach. The car hit some rocks.... He was killed instantly.''

Her fingers gripped the coffee mug with white-knuckled force, belying the calm of her recitation. Gage stared at the tabletop, searching for something to say and finding his mind blank of everything but denial. He simply couldn't equate the story she'd just told him with Rick. Not his best friend, not the man who'd been as close to him as any of his brothers.

"I know it's hard to take in," Kelsey said. She reached across the table to touch the back of his hand. Gage lifted his eyes to her face and realized that *she* was trying to comfort *him*.

He shifted his hand to hold hers. "All the way home, I kept hoping I'd get here and find out that it was all a mistake, that Cole had gotten it wrong."

"Every morning, when I wake up, there's a few seconds where I think it's all a horrible nightmare," Kelsey whispered, staring at their joined hands.

They sat without speaking, linked by the touch of their hands, linked by their grief. Gage didn't know how much time passed before the rattle of the lid on the soup pan broke the silence.

"Your soup's hot," Kelsey said, relieved to have a distraction.

While Gage ate soup he didn't want, they talked of trivial things, avoiding, by unspoken agreement, the topic uppermost in both their minds. There didn't really seem to be anything else to say. Rick was gone, and both their lives were forever changed.

Gage woke from a restless sleep, aware that something was not right. He hadn't been sleeping well, but it wasn't because it was a strange bed. He'd stayed with Rick and Kelsey before, which made this bed as familiar as any. Because his work as a structural engineer kept him out of the country most of the time, he'd never bothered to establish a home base and he'd learned to sleep anywhere, including a lot of places where a bed was an unheard-of luxury.

Kelsey had insisted that he stay in the guest room, just as he usually did, but this was one time when familiarity was not a comfort. His mind had churned with thoughts of how much everything had changed since he'd last slept in this room. It had been after midnight when he dozed off, and a glance at the clock told him that it was almost two o'clock now.

He lay in the narrow bed, staring up at the darkened ceiling, trying to place what had awakened him. Had it been a sound? Maybe little Danny was awake and not happy about it. If that was it, perhaps he could deal with whatever the boy's problem was before he woke Kelsey. It was doubtful that she'd been getting much sleep lately.

Gage swung his legs out of bed, reaching for the jeans he'd draped over the foot of the bed. Out of habit, he shook them out before stepping into them. Years of working in less hospitable climates had taught him to be wary of multilegged creatures who might find his clothing an inviting vacation spot. The rasp of the zipper sounded loud. The house was so quiet now that he wondered if he'd imagined the sound that had awakened him. But he was awake now and he might as well investigate. On his way out of the room, he tugged on a flannel shirt.

Barefoot, he padded down the hallway to Danny's room. Easing open the door, he stepped inside and walked silently over to the crib. Whatever had awak-

ened him, it obviously hadn't been Danny. The boy
slept with the sweet abandon of childhood, flat on his
back, arms flung out to his sides, eyes scrunched shut,
his mouth slightly open.

Smiling a little, Gage reached down and tugged
loose the cartoon-printed blanket that was twisted beneath Danny's small body. He eased it up over the
child and then reached out to smooth a lock of white
gold hair back from the boy's forehead.

He'd been in California when Daniel was born and
he'd never forgotten the way he'd felt when Rick had
asked him to be godfather to the tiny newborn—elation and panic in equal measure. He'd tried to refuse.

*"I can't." Gage looked at Rick as if he'd grown a
second head.*

"Sure you can," Rick said firmly.

*"There's no one else we'd rather have," Kelsey
added.*

*Gage transferred his panicked gaze to her. She sat
on the sofa, holding her son. Ridiculous, Gage
thought, letting something that small out of the hospital. Not to mention letting Kelsey come home the
day after giving birth. Surely it couldn't be good for
her to be out of bed so soon. Why hadn't Rick insisted she stay in the hospital or at least stay in bed for
a week or two? But then, obviously Rick had lost his
mind or he wouldn't have suggested something as
crazy as this.*

*"I can't," Gage said again. He looked at Rick, his
eyes demanding an end to this scene. Rick was one of
the few people who knew the truth. He should understand how impossible this was. But there was no
yielding in his friend's eyes.*

"*Give it up, buddy. You're going to be a godfather, whether you like it or not.*"

"*There are people better suited to the responsibility,*" Gage said, trying to sound casual. Was it possible that Rick had forgotten? That he didn't remember why Gage was the last person on earth he should ask to be a godfather to his son?

"*No, there isn't,*" Kelsey said firmly. She stood up, and it was all Gage could do to keep from demanding that she sit down—that she lie down, for God's sake. She closed the small distance between them and looked up at him with those clear gray eyes that always seemed to see so much more than they should. "*Gage Walker, meet your godson.*"

She held out the blanket-wrapped bundle, and Gage took it from her before he had a chance to realize what he was doing. He would have thrust the baby back immediately, but she foiled his intention by returning to her seat on the sofa.

Against his will, Gage looked down at the baby. Daniel Richard Jackson was asleep, his face screwed up in that peculiarly intense expression of newborns, as if life, even sleeping, required all his concentration.

Gage shifted his hold, automatically cradling the tiny body in the crook of his arm. It had been years since he held a baby. Not since—his thoughts shied away from the last time he'd held a baby. He didn't want to think about that.

Godfather. The word seemed to carry a huge burden of responsibility. Maybe it didn't mean what it had in times past, but he knew, if he agreed to the title, he'd feel obliged to assume the responsibilities that went with it. And Rick knew it, too, damn him. Knew,

*as well, that there was no way that Gage could turn
him down. Double damn him.*

As if sensing his friend's capitulation, Rick laughed.

*"Hey, don't look so glum. It isn't like I'm going to
keel over and leave you to raise my kid." He grinned,
his eyes holding understanding and a trace of laughter. He knew exactly what was going through Gage's
mind and he was making it clear that he wasn't going
to let Gage off the hook. "I have every intention of
being around for a very long time."*

The memory brought a bittersweet edge to Gage's
smile. Would Rick have been so blasé about choosing
his son's godfather if he'd been able to see into the
future and know that he wasn't going to be around;
that Danny was going to need someone to provide
more than an occasional birthday present and a pat on
the head?

"Dammit, Rick, you should have thought about
this," Gage whispered, his eyes on the sleeping child.
"You knew better than anyone what a lousy choice I
was. Why didn't you choose someone else?"

There was no answer, only the soft hiss of the rain
falling outside. And underlying that, a repetition of
the sound that had awakened him. This time he recognized it for what it was. With a quick glance at
Danny, Gage left the bedroom, pulling the door almost shut behind him. He hesitated in the hallway.
Maybe he should just go back to bed and pretend he
hadn't heard anything.

Even as the thought occurred to him, he knew he
couldn't do it. He could no more walk away from the
sound of Kelsey crying than he could leap tall buildings in a single bound. With a muttered prayer that he

wasn't making a mistake, he turned toward the front of the house.

Gage paused in the doorway of the living room, letting his eyes adjust to the darkness. Kelsey was sitting on one end of the sofa, her arms wrapped around her knees and her face buried in the pale blue flannel of her robe as if to muffle her sobs.

"Kelsey." He spoke her name quietly, but her body jerked as if he'd shouted. She lifted her head from her knees but didn't look in his direction.

"Gage! Did I...did I wake you?" Her breath hitched in the middle of the question. "I'm sorry."

"You didn't wake me," he said, only half lying. He hadn't been sleeping well anyway. "Are you okay?"

Stupid question, Walker. Of course she's not okay.

"No. I mean, yes. I'm okay." The way her breath caught on a stifled sob after every other word made the reassurance less than effective.

"Do you want to be alone?"

"If you don't mind. I'm not very good company right now." She wiped her hands across her face.

"I wasn't expecting to be entertained," he said dryly.

"I know." She sniffed. "I just don't want to inflict this on anyone." She sniffed again. "Stupid," she muttered, as much to herself as to him. "Please go, Gage."

"All right." He turned to leave but stopped when he heard her sniff again. There was a box of tissues on a little table near the doorway. Picking it up, he carried it over to the sofa and set the box down on the end table next to Kelsey. "Here."

"Th-thank you."

He saw her reach for a tissue as he was turning away. It seemed as if there should be something more he could do, some comfort he could offer. A box of tissues hardly seemed like enough.

"Gage?"

"Yeah?" He turned in the doorway, seeing her face only as a pale blur in the darkness. She didn't say anything, and he wondered if he'd imagined her saying his name. "Kelsey?"

"Don't go." The words were hardly even a whisper. "I . . . don't want to be alone."

"You're not." Gage was across the room in two quick strides, and she came into his arms with a sob that seemed to explode from the depths of her soul.

He held her while she cried, wrapping his arms around her and rocking her a little, her pain echoing his own. He almost envied her tears. Maybe tears would help dissolve the knot in his chest.

"It's going to be all right," he murmured without conviction.

Kelsey didn't cry long. Within minutes she was choking her tears into silence, her breath catching in awkward little half-sobs as she fought for control. She lay against him like a tired child.

"I should have waited up," she said, struggling to speak through her tears.

"For what?"

"For Rick. That night. I should have waited up for him. He . . . told me not to wait up for him, and I went . . . to bed but I should have stayed up."

"It wouldn't have made any difference."

"I was *asleep* when it happened!" Her tone made it a crime.

"It wouldn't have changed anything, Kelsey."

"I shouldn't have been asleep. I should have known something was wrong. I shouldn't have just slept through it."

Gage brushed her hair back from her forehead and wished, for the hundredth time, that he could find the right words.

"It's only in books and movies that people always know when someone they love is in trouble. In real life it doesn't work like that."

"I should have known," she insisted stubbornly.

"If Rick were here, what do you think he'd tell you?" Gage asked with sudden inspiration. "You know how much he believed in ESP and psychic stuff."

"He didn't believe in it at all," Kelsey corrected him. "He thought it was ridiculous."

"'If I can't see it, touch it or smell it, it don't exist,'" Gage quoted, adopting Rick's most dogmatic tone of voice. Kelsey's strangled spurt of laughter encouraged him that he was on the right track. "The man barely believed in electricity."

"And he thought radio was a trick," Kelsey added.

"I think he was half convinced that there were little people inside the television set," Gage said, and was rewarded with a watery chuckle.

"I guess he wouldn't have thought much of my idea that I should have known something was wrong, would he?" Kelsey said slowly.

"He'd have said you were crazy," Gage confirmed cheerfully.

"I guess he would have. I suppose he would have been right."

"For once I'd have to agree with him," Gage told her, keeping his tone deliberately light.

"Thanks," Kelsey said dryly. "I'm sorry I cried all over you."

"Nothing wrong with crying." Gage reached over her head and yanked half a dozen tissues out of the box. "Dry your eyes and blow your nose," he ordered as handed them to her.

At another time, Kelsey might have protested his autocratic tone. She'd never been much good at taking orders. But right now, it felt so good to simply lie against him and feel not quite so alone.

"Were you sleeping out here?" he asked, glancing at the pillow shoved against the arm of the sofa and the blanket that dragged half on the sofa, half on the floor.

"I can't sleep in our... in the bedroom," she said, her voice husky from too many tears and too little sleep. "I tried, but when I wake up, I forget and I...sometimes I think he's going to be there."

"You can't spend the rest of your life on the sofa."

"No." Kelsey's voice quavered a little at the reminder that it was the rest of her life they were talking about. "Damn," she muttered, dabbing impatiently at the tears that sprang to her eyes. "I swore I wasn't going to cry anymore."

"Nothing wrong with crying," Gage said again. "Not unless you've already cried enough to float the *Queen Mary.*"

"I don't know that there's a maximum limit on tears."

"If there is, I'm sure I've exceeded it," Kelsey murmured.

She really should sit up, she thought, stifling a yawn. Gage was probably anxious to get back to bed. But it felt so good to lean against him, to feel as if, for a little while at least, she didn't have to be strong, didn't have to be alone. She was so tired of being strong. So very, very tired...

Gage waited until he was sure Kelsey was asleep and then waited a little while longer, listening to the quiet rhythm of her breathing. He eased away slowly, careful not to wake her as he moved off the sofa, shifting her to lie on the cushions. Her sleep was the heavy slumber of exhaustion, and she didn't stir when he pulled the blanket over her, tucking it around her shoulders.

He stood looking down at her for a long time, his eyes shadowed. He finally turned and left her alone, going back to his room, where he lay awake until the gray light of dawn crept through the curtains.

Chapter 2

Kelsey woke to the sound of high-pitched giggles, mixed with the deeper note of masculine laughter. She was caught between sleep and waking, her mouth curved in a smile. She must have overslept, and Rick was making Danny's breakfast and undoubtedly making a mess at the same time. He couldn't seem to set foot in a kitchen without leaving behind a disaster.

He laughed again, the sound deeper and less familiar than it should have been. She frowned, struggling to hold on to the remnants of sleep. But they slipped away like tattered wraiths dissipating before a brisk wind. The same wind that brought memory sweeping back.

Rick. Oh, God. Rick. She squeezed her eyes tight shut. The pain was there, waiting for her, just as it had been every morning since the accident. First there was denial—a part of her insisting that it was all a terrible nightmare. And then there was acceptance—he was gone forever. And then the emptiness—deep, hollow, aching emptiness.

It would get better, she told herself, repeating the words of comfort so many people had offered. Time would make it easier. She hadn't been left alone. She still had Danny.

Danny! Kelsey's eyes flew open, and she shot upright on the sofa, her heart thumping with panic. Oh, God, how could she have overslept when Rick wasn't here anymore? Their son had only her now, and she'd virtually left him alone. As if on cue, the laughter came again—Danny's giggle, rich and fat with the pure joy of childhood and the deeper rumble of a man's chuckle.

Gage. Kelsey relaxed against the sofa, letting her heartbeat gradually slow to normal. Gage was here. He was taking care of Danny. And entertaining him pretty well, from the sound of it, she thought, hearing her son laugh again.

Kelsey felt her cheeks warm when she remembered the way she'd begged Gage to stay with her and then sobbed on his chest like a baby. But her embarrassment was only momentary. She didn't have to be embarrassed with Gage.

She shoved her fingers through her hair, combing it into a vague semblance of order. Standing, she stretched to ease the kinks in her back before starting for the kitchen. If Gage didn't mind keeping an eye on Danny for a little while, maybe she'd take a long, hot bath later—an indulgence that was impossible now unless she was willing to have Danny and a flotilla of rubber toys join her in the tub.

But when she broached the possibility to Gage a few minutes later, he shook his head.

"We won't have time for that kind of thing today," he said firmly.

"We won't?" Kelsey lifted her eyes from the plate he'd just set in front of her and gave him a surprised look. "Why not?"

"We've got a lot to do. Danny and I have mapped out a battle plan, haven't we, short stuff?"

Danny nodded, his mouth too full of scrambled egg to do anything more.

"A battle plan for what?" Kelsey asked, glancing from her son to Gage, who sat across the table from her.

"Eat your breakfast and I'll tell you."

"I'm not really—"

"How do you expect Danny to appreciate the importance of proper nutrition in the morning if his own mother does nothing but swill coffee?" he interrupted before she could say that she wasn't hungry.

"I think he's a little young to be worrying about nutrition. And I do not *swill* coffee!"

"If you say so," he said, looking dubious. "But you're going to need plenty of protein and carbohydrates if you want to keep up with the two of us today, right, buddy?"

"Uh-huh." Danny's enthusiastic agreement was muffled by his eggs.

"Tell your mom she'd better eat her breakfast if she doesn't want to get left in the dust," Gage said as he mopped eggs off the boy's face.

Kelsey started to tell him that she wasn't hungry. Her appetite hadn't been particularly good lately. But the bacon did smell pretty good, and he'd scrambled mushrooms and green onions into the eggs, which were fluffy and moist. He'd gone to a lot of trouble. It would be rude not to at least taste it.

Twenty minutes later, she avoided Gage's smug look as she handed him her empty plate. To his credit, he didn't say anything but he didn't have to. His expression practically shouted *I told you so.*

"Go put on some jeans. We've got work to do."

Kelsey started to ask what he was talking about but swallowed the words. He seemed to be enjoying the air of mystery. Why spoil his fun?

Half an hour later, she wasn't feeling quite so magnanimous.

"I don't think I'm ready for this, Gage."

"You can't sleep on the couch forever, Kelsey."

"It's not forever. It's only been a few weeks," she protested.

"That's a few weeks more than Rick would have wanted you to be miserable. Come on, I'm not talking about erasing every sign of him from the house. I'm just suggesting that we move you into the spare bedroom and turn this room into a study."

The two of them stood in the hallway outside the master bedroom. Danny sat on the floor next to them, running a toy car across the floor, using the boards in the hardwood floor as lanes on his imaginary highway.

"I don't think I can," Kelsey said, glancing uneasily through the door at the room she and Rick had shared.

"You said you couldn't sleep in there. And since you've moved a bunch of your clothes into Danny's room, I assume you don't even want to go inside."

"I'll get over it."

"Why should you? If I remember correctly, you didn't like this room for a master bedroom to start with. You said you liked to wake up with the sun in your eyes. The spare room is on the east side of the house," he elaborated in case she might not have realized it.

"Rick liked this room, though."

"Because it was on the north side and as far away from the sun as it's possible to get. I always suspected he was half vampire."

"He wasn't much of a morning person," Kelsey agreed. But her smile was fleeting. She glanced through the open door again. "I'm not sure I'm ready for this, Gage."

"There's no reason to wait," he stated implacably.

"It hasn't been that long!" she said angrily.

Kelsey could feel him looking at her but she kept her eyes on her son, seeing him through a film of tears. Gage didn't say anything for a moment, leaving only the sound of Danny's growled car noises to break the silence.

"I don't want to upset you, Kelsey," Gage said at last, his voice low and quiet. "I just think you need to start trying to get on with life. You and I both know it's what Rick would want."

He was right. She knew he was right. Rick had never been one to hold on to the past, not even for a moment. She was the one who loved old houses, antique furniture, scrapbooks, musty attics and putting down roots. Rick would have been perfectly content to live in a condo, move every year and own nothing that was more than a few months old. *Looking back is a waste of time.* She'd heard him say those words a hundred times.

"He'd be the first to urge you to move on," Gage said, reading her mind.

"Too bad he's not here to do that," she snapped. She lifted her head to glare at him. "But he's not here, and I'm not going to forget him overnight just to make him happy."

There was a pause while Gage tried to sort through the tangled web of her reasoning. Kelsey replayed her words in her head, heard their absurdity and closed her eyes briefly in embarrassment.

"So, what you're saying is that you're going to be miserable as long as you want, just to spite Rick?" Gage drawled slowly.

"I really hate you," she said on a sigh. She looked at him, seeing the smile in his eyes and the understanding beneath it. "You're obnoxious and irritating."

"And right?" He emphasized the question with a lift of his dark brows.

Kelsey hesitated, her eyes shifting away from him to the bedroom. He was right. It was time to start picking up the pieces of her life, for Danny's sake if not for her own. It was just so hard to think of letting go, even a little bit. As long as she held tight to the pain, it was as if Rick were still a part of her life.

"What about you? If I move into the spare room, where are you going to sleep?" It was a last-ditch effort to delay the inevitable, and the tilt of Gage's eyebrow told her that he recognized it as such.

"I'll sleep on the sofa."

"You're too tall," she said triumphantly, having anticipated his answer. "You'd be miserable. And I wouldn't be able to sleep, knowing you weren't comfortable."

"Kelsey." Gage caught her hands, making her aware that she'd been waving them up and down as if trying to take flight. "I've slept on much worse beds than your sofa. I'll be fine."

She started to argue, caught his eye and closed her mouth without speaking. She felt a movement against her leg and looked down at Danny, who was now standing next to her, running his car up and down the seam of her jeans. He grinned when he saw her looking at him, his small face full of love and trust. The past few weeks had been hard on him. He missed Rick, and no matter how hard she tried to keep it from him, he had to sense her own unhappiness. She ruffled her fingers through his silky blond hair and then lifted her head to look at Gage, her chin set with determination.

"Where do we start?"

"You didn't have to get up to see me off." Gage frowned down at Kelsey.

"I wanted to." They'd had the same argument the night before, with Gage insisting that there was no need for her to see him off and Kelsey equally determined to be up to tell him goodbye.

She was sitting at the kitchen table, her hands wrapped around a cup of coffee. It was the early hours of the morning, the sun not even a glimmer on the eastern horizon. Around them the house was silent, a sure indication that Danny was sound asleep. When he was awake, silence was generally nonexistent.

Gage was leaning against the counter, working on his second cup of coffee. He'd refused her offer of breakfast—he'd eat on the plane. In a few minutes, he was leaving, going back to South America to finish the job he'd interrupted to come to California.

"Are you sure you're going to be all right?" he asked.

"I'm sure," she assured him patiently, though it was at least the third time he'd asked the question in the past half hour. He'd spent the past two weeks convincing her that she could move past Rick's death and start a new life, but now that he was leaving, he seemed suddenly uneasy.

You and me both, Kelsey thought, keeping her expression serene. She'd always thought of herself as an independent woman but she was fighting the urge to grab hold of his sleeve and cling like ivy on a wall.

"I'll be fine," she assured him in a tone so even that she almost fooled herself.

Gage looked doubtful but thankfully he didn't express his doubts out loud. If he had, she might have broken down and begged him not to leave.

"You'll call if you need anything." The words were more of an order than a request.

"I'll call," she promised, but apparently she didn't sound sincere enough.

"I mean it," he said insistently. "If there's anything you need, you know how to get a message to me. It might take a while, but I'll get back to you as soon as I can."

"I know you will."

"Anything." He gave the word heavy emphasis, his eyes intent on hers.

"Stop worrying," she said, half laughing. "I'm a big girl, Gage. I can take care of myself. And Danny."

"Yeah." But he didn't look reassured. He ran his fingers through his hair and then kneaded his fingers against the nape of his neck, his dark brows coming together, shadowing the blue of his eyes.

"Stop worrying about me, Gage," she said again. She got up and moved around the table, setting her hand on his sleeve, feeling the solid warmth of muscle beneath the blue chambray.

Solid. That's the one word she most associated with Gage Walker. Rock solid. God knows, she'd needed that solidity. She'd been drowning before he came, drowning in grief and fear. And he'd given her something solid to hold on to. He'd shared her grief and bullied her out of her fear and convinced her—almost—that life was going to continue. Not life as she'd known it, but life nevertheless. He'd not only held her when she cried, he'd made her laugh, something she'd half believed she'd never do again. He'd rearranged her house, played with her son and made her look ahead rather than back.

"I'm going to miss you," she admitted, tilting her head back to look up at him.

"I bet." He gave her a lopsided grin. "I've harassed you for two solid weeks. I'm surprised you didn't throw me out a long time ago."

"I considered it a time or two," she admitted. "But Danny likes you."

"The kid's got great taste."

"He's going to miss you," Kelsey said, her smile fading as she considered how much her small son had lost recently.

"I'll be back," Gage said.

"I know." But a month could seem like a century when you were two. She saw the concern in Gage's eyes and smiled again. She didn't want him worrying about them any more than he already was. "I'll just have time to repair some of the damage you've done spoiling him," she said lightly.

Gage smiled. "It's my duty as his godfather to spoil him." His smile faded, and the intensity was back in his eyes. "There's something I need to ask you before I go. I've been trying to find a tactful way to ask it and I haven't, so I guess I'll just spit it out."

"What?" The look Kelsey gave him held a touch of alarm. He looked so serious.

"Are you doing okay for money?"

The question sounded just as blunt and intrusive as he'd thought it would. Kelsey flushed and seemed to draw into herself in some subtle way.

"I know you want to tell me it's none of my business," he continued before she had a chance to speak. "And ordinarily I'd agree with you and I'd throw me out on my ear. But I am Danny's godfather, so I've got a right to be concerned about his welfare. Besides, Rick asked me to take care of you."

Which was true enough even if Rick had been three sheets to the wind at the time and he'd always been given to getting a little maudlin when he drank.

"Contrary to recent appearances, I'm not completely helpless." Her tone was even, revealing nothing of what she was thinking.

Caution suggested that he let the topic drop. But concern for her welfare was too strong.

"I know you're not helpless. I'm just trying to make sure you're not broke," he said bluntly.

Pride had stiffened her spine, but she couldn't prevent a snort of laughter from escaping her. "Very tactfully put, Gage."

His smile held a rueful twist. "Tact isn't one of my strong suits."

"No kidding." Kelsey couldn't hold on to her annoyance. How could she be angry with him for worrying about her? "I'm not going to let you give me money."

"Why not? I'm not rich but I make a pretty good salary and I don't have much to spend it on. I've got a little put away. You're—" He broke off when Kelsey put her hand on his arm again.

"I'm not going to take your money." She said it slowly and distinctly, leaving no room to doubt her sincerity.

"If you need it..."

Kelsey was already shaking her head. She thought briefly of the frighteningly small amount of money in her bank account, but there were some things that just couldn't be compromised.

"I don't," she said firmly. "Thank you for the offer, but I don't need your money."

"If you're sure." He didn't look happy, but Kelsey wouldn't give in just to make him feel better.

"I'm sure," she lied. "You'd better get out of here if you don't want to miss your plane," she continued briskly.

Gage glanced at the clock that hung over the doorway. "You're right." He downed the last of his coffee, grimacing at the lukewarm taste of it.

Kelsey followed him into the entryway, swallowing against the lump in her throat as she watched him pick up his duffel bag. He turned to look at her, his expression unreadable in the dim light.

"If you need anything..." he began.

"You'll be the first to know," she interrupted.

"Have I said that before?"

"Only about a thousand times."

"You're exaggerating. I bet it's barely seven hundred and fifty."

"Eight hundred, at the very least." Kelsey's smile shook around the edges.

"I'm about to make it eight hundred and one," Gage said. "Call if you need me, and I'll get here as soon as I can."

"I will," she promised.

They stood there, looking at each other, reluctant, now that the moment had arrived, to say goodbye. Kelsey moved first, stepping forward to slide her arms around his waist and pressing her cheek to his chest. Gage put his free arm around her and hugged her tight.

"You're going to be all right," he told her fiercely.

Kelsey couldn't force her voice past the lump in her throat but she managed to nod. A part of her believed she *was* going to be all right. But there was another part of her—a small, frightened little girl—that was terrified by the thought of his leaving, terrified to be alone with her memories.

With an effort, she forced herself to step away from him. "Get out of here," she said, pleased to hear that her voice was almost steady.

"Don't forget—"

"I won't!" Her laugh was a little damp around the edges. She waved her hands in shooing motions. "Go away before you drive me crazy!"

"You can always call Cole if you need anything," he reminded her, mentioning his brother.

"I know, I know." She went around him to open the front door. *"Out!"*

Gage grinned. "You have the number for the head office," he said, taking a step toward the door.

"I have more numbers than the phone book!" Kelsey gave a choke of laughter. "I'm not going to need any of them."

"Maybe I should give them to you again, just in case," he began.

"Maybe you should go before I throttle you with my bare hands," she threatened, laughing, just as he'd intended her to.

"If you're going to get nasty about it," he said, drawing his mouth down in a hurt expression. He was standing on the porch by now.

"I am," she promised. "If you give me one more number or tell me one more time to call if I need you, I won't be responsible for my actions."

"Then I guess I'd better go because I'm feeling an uncontrollable urge to give you the number for—"

"Goodbye, Gage!"

Laughing, Kelsey shut the door on his grinning face. But her laughter faded as soon as she heard his footsteps moving off the porch. With her eyes shut, she leaned back against the door and listened. She winced at the sound of his car door shutting and winced again when the engine started. A moment later, she heard the car pull away from the curb.

He was gone.

And she was alone again.

Chapter 3

Three Years Later

"Mama! Mama!"

Kelsey was crouched on her hands and knees next to a row of snap peas, carefully picking the ripe pods and dropping them in the shallow basket beside her. At the sound of Danny's urgent cry, she stood and looked over the top of the trellised pea vines, shading her eyes against the sun so that she could see her son. He was running toward her across the garden, his short legs churning with the excitement.

"I'm over here, baby," she called out, waving her hand to help him find her.

He wasn't really a baby anymore, she thought, watching him dart among the carefully laid out beds of vegetables. He'd be five in a few short weeks, ready to start school this next fall. He was growing so fast.

She had the whimsical thought that if she could get him to hold still long enough, she could actually watch him grow. Not that she'd ever get the chance to try that particular experiment, she thought as he skidded to a halt in front of her, practically dancing with excitement. *Still* was not in Danny's vocabulary.

"Uncle Gage," he managed to say, too excited or too breathless to say more.

"Gage?" Kelsey glanced toward the house, half expecting to see Gage's tall figure walking toward her. But there was nothing between her and the house except the beds of lush greenery she cultivated. "Did he call?"

"He's coming!" Danny rocked back and forth, his red sneakers bouncing on the pathway.

"He missed Christmas," she said, thinking it was a shame he hadn't been able to get home for the holiday.

"We still got his peasant," Danny reminded her.

"Present," she corrected automatically.

"I bet he'll have peasants for us, too," he continued, oblivious to his mother's vocabulary lesson. "We can have Christmas again!"

Kelsey smiled at his simple summation of life.

"I'm sure Uncle Gage would like that," she said, reaching out to ruffle her fingers through his flaxen hair. "Did he say when he was going to be here?"

Danny's small face wrinkled in thought, only to clear a moment later. He nodded. "Thursday."

This was Monday. Three days. That gave her time to give his room a quick cleaning, put fresh sheets on the bed and some flowers on the bureau.

"Danny!" The call came from the direction of the house.

Kelsey waved to the teenager who stood on the porch. Susan McCallister was the daughter of one of Kelsey's neighbors. She came over every day after school and kept an eye on Danny for a couple of hours. Kelsey had been relieved when Susan agreed to continue her baby-sitting chores during the Christmas vacation. Much as she loved her son, she was grateful for the chance to spend uninterrupted time working in the gardens that had supplied most of their income for the past year.

"I bet Susan has a snack ready for you," she told Danny.

"Cookies!" The gleeful shout was tossed over his shoulder as he spun around and charged full tilt for the house.

Kelsey watched until she saw him reach the house, rushing up the steps and bursting through the door as if he feared the cookies might vanish if he didn't get to them quickly. Awed as always by the amount of energy contained in her son's small person, Kelsey knelt back down and continued with the task he'd interrupted.

She'd promised to deliver the sugar snaps to a restaurant in Santa Barbara before four so they could serve them for dinner that night. Her hands moving automatically, she worked her way down the row, letting her mind wander.

She'd worked hard these past two years, cultivating a market for her organically grown fresh produce as carefully as she cultivated the produce itself. There hadn't been many options open to a single mother who wanted to stay home with her son. After giving it some thought, she'd come up with the idea of putting her love of gardening to work. It had turned out better than she'd ever dared to hope. Now she could sell as much as she could grow, and the income was enough, with a little care, for her and Danny to live on. And the money Gage gave her for his room nicely closed any gaps in her income.

Kelsey frowned, thinking about her arrangement with Gage. Even after more than two years, she still wasn't comfortable with it. She didn't like taking charity, and though Gage would argue until he turned blue in the face, that was exactly what it was. Rent! As if Gage would ever have to pay rent to stay in her home!

She pulled a snap pea loose with a yank that made the vine rustle in protest. Offering a mental apology to the plant, she tugged another pod loose in a more decorous fashion. Her jaw tightened with remembered annoyance.

Gage had come home again about six months after Rick's accident. Though Kelsey hadn't said anything to him, he must have guessed that money was tight. She'd sold her relatively new car and bought a much older model, and she'd seen the skepticism in his eyes when she mumbled some excuse about an older car being less vulnerable to theft. Even without her selling the car, he'd probably been able to guess that Rick hadn't left much by way of insurance. Rick hadn't been one to plan too far ahead. Besides, at their age, who thought about dying?

With a sigh, Kelsey sat back on her heels and stared at the wall of vines in front of her. She felt a hundred years older than she had three years ago. There was nothing like being left a widow *and* broke to make you grow up fast. She'd seen firsthand just how quickly a life could be snuffed out. She'd never again take the future for granted.

Gage had known Rick well enough to guess something of the situation she was in and he'd come up with the idea that he could rent a room from her.

"It'd be nice to have a place to come home to, but I'm not around enough to keep an apartment going. It wouldn't make sense. If you'd rent me a room, though, that would be perfect." He gave her look that could only be called wistful.

"You don't have to rent a room from me," she protested, confused by his suggestion. *"You're always welcome here. You know that."*

"I appreciate that but I'd be more comfortable if we made it official. Otherwise, I'd feel like I was taking advantage of you."

"Don't be ridiculous." She set down the pruning shears she'd been using to nip back an overly rambunctious bougainvillea and turned fully to face him. He was working on a loose board on the porch but he put down the hammer and tilted his head to look up at her.

"You're family, Gage. Danny and I both love having you here." She gestured to where her son was diligently—and vigorously—pounding on the porch step with a plastic hammer, in obvious imitation of Gage's activity.

"I appreciate that, Kelsey, but I just wouldn't feel comfortable staying here when I'm home unless you'll let me pay rent. I've checked around and I think I've come up with a fair rent." He named a sum that made Kelsey's eyes widen.

"Are you kidding? You don't really think I'm going to take that kind of money from you, do you?"

"It's a fair rent," he insisted.

"For where? Beverly Hills? Not that it matters," she added quickly, "because I'm not going to take money from you anyway."

He didn't say anything for a moment, and she thought she'd succeeded in ending the discussion. But she'd underestimated him.

"It's too bad," he said slowly. "I was hoping we could work something out. I'll give Mom a call a little later. I know I can stay with her."

"You mean you won't stay here if I won't agree to charge you rent?" she demanded incredulously.

"I wouldn't be comfortable otherwise," he said with a bland regret that made her want to hit him, preferably with something large and very hard.

"I know what this is about," she informed him, resentment simmering in her voice. "You think I need money so you've come up with this ridiculous scheme to give me some."

Gage raised his brows, his blue eyes widening with surprise. "You told me you didn't need money. Why wouldn't I believe you?"

Because I was lying and you know it. But of course she couldn't say that.

"Besides," he continued coolly, "you said you'd let me know if you needed anything, including money."

Kelsey was torn between the urge to scream and the need to cry, a feeling that had become all too familiar these past few months. Just when she thought she'd regained her emotional balance, something happened to show her just how fragile that balance was.

"I don't want you paying me rent," she said, aware that she sounded more sulky than firm.

"And I couldn't be comfortable otherwise," he replied just as firmly.

Neither of them spoke for a space of time. Danny filled the silence with the ragged thunk of his hammer as he tried to pound a purple plastic screw into the porch floor.

Kelsey was trapped and she knew it. She knew Gage well enough to know he wasn't going to back away from this. Which left her two choices: she could give in graciously and allow him to help her or she could stand by her pride and he'd spend the remainder of his time off at his mother's house.

She didn't want him to go. Having him here made the house seem a little less empty, made her life seem a little less empty. And Danny adored him.

"I can't take that much," she muttered. It was not exactly a gracious acceptance but it was the best she could manage.

Kelsey shook her head, remembering the conversation. At least Gage had had the good sense not to look smug. She'd been so annoyed, she just might have hauled off and belted him one. And the money had been a godsend, she had to admit. It had meant the difference between her and Danny's being able to live in reasonable comfort and barely scraping by.

But things had changed in the past two years. Her business was solid, as reliable as anything that depended on the whims of Mother Nature could possibly be, and she had a few thousand dollars tucked away as insurance against a rainy day. Or, in her case, an unexpected frost or freak hailstorm—neither likely possibilities in an area that went years without seeing temperatures much below thirty degrees.

Kelsey stood, dusting off the knees of her jeans before she bent to pick up the basket of snap peas. She was going to have to talk to Gage when he came home this time, explain to him that it was no longer necessary to keep up this pretense of his paying her rent.

Thursday. She felt a glow of pleasure at the thought of seeing him again. Life always seemed just a little more interesting when Gage was around. She brushed her hair back from her face. Maybe she'd see about getting her hair cut between now and Thursday. It was getting a little shaggy.

Humming under her breath, she headed for the house.

Kelsey woke abruptly, coming out of a sound sleep to darkness and the awareness that something was wrong. She lay on her back, staring up at the ceiling, trying to place what had awakened her. A noise, maybe? As if on cue, she heard it again, a scratchy squeaking sound. The sound was both familiar and frightening. Familiar because she heard it every time she walked across the living room and stepped on the loose floorboard next to the sofa. Frightening because she shouldn't be hearing it in the middle of the night.

Danny! Kelsey shot up, tossing the covers aside. Pausing only to snatch up the baseball bat she kept under the edge of the bed, she dashed across the bedroom, barefoot and silent. It was probably nothing, she was telling herself as she eased open the bedroom door and crept out into the hall. It was an old house; it could be just the natural sounds as the building settled and shifted, sinking more comfortably onto its foundations. Nothing to panic about. Certainly nothing to put her heart so solidly in her throat.

She paused in front of Danny's half-open door. The soft glow of the night-light was enough to reveal her son's sturdy body sprawled across his bed, the covers kicked off as usual. Whatever she'd heard, it hadn't been enough to disturb Danny, but then, short of a minor explosion next to his ear, not much did wake him. He always had been a solid sleeper.

A muffled thud from the front of the house had her heart in her throat again. She eased the bedroom door shut, closing her son away from the danger—if there was any danger, she reminded herself. The thud had probably been an animal, maybe a raccoon jumping onto the porch roof or a skunk knocking over a potted plant during his nightly search for dinner.

But the reassurances did nothing to slow the pounding of her heart as she crept down the hall toward the living room. Nothing to be afraid of, she reminded herself. The house had been locked up tight before she went to bed. Besides, crime, while not unheard-of around here, was a fairly rare thing. Just an animal, she told herself firmly as she eased her head around the edge of the doorjamb and peeked into the living room.

And found herself staring at a broad—very broad—male back.

Kelsey's heart stopped completely and then started again with a thunk that seemed to knock the breath from her. Idiot! The word screamed in her head. What was she doing, creeping around in the middle of the night armed with a baseball bat? Who did she think she was? Rambo? Why hadn't she picked up the

phone in her bedroom and dialed 911, as any sane
woman would have done?

She slid one foot back. There was a phone in the
kitchen....

But her caution came too late. Or perhaps her retreat wasn't as silent as she'd hoped. Because the intruder turned suddenly. Kelsey reacted instinctively to
protect herself. She jabbed the baseball bat in the direction of his midsection. Either she misjudged or he
deflected her attack, because she felt the end of the bat
hit something much harder than a stomach. His grunt
of pain told her that she'd connected, but the speed
with which he moved told her she hadn't landed a dis-
abling blow.

Kelsey squeaked with dismay as the bat was jerked
out of her hands. By the time it thudded to the floor,
she'd already turned to run. But he was too quick for
her. Hard fingers closed around her arm, and her own
momentum had her spinning toward him. She might
have screamed, but her breath was momentarily
knocked out of her when she collided with a wall of
solid muscle.

He was too big, too strong. A wave of pure feminine terror washed over her. He could do anything he
wanted with her, and she'd be helpless to stop him.
And then she remembered her son, sleeping peace-
fully just a few feet away and she felt adrenaline pump
new strength into her. She gathered herself to struggle
and suddenly heard the sound of her name.

"Kelsey! It's me. Gage."

"Gage?" She stared up at him, her heart thudding
so hard it was difficult to speak. Her voice rose on a
disbelieving squeak. "Gage?"

"It's me," he confirmed. He reached out to switch on a table lamp, banishing the shadows to the corners of the room.

"Gage. Oh, God." The adrenaline faded abruptly, leaving her light-headed.

Gage felt her sway and quickly slid one arm around her waist, bracing her against the length of his body as her knees threatened to give out on her. His other arm throbbed dully from the blow she'd dealt him with the baseball bat that now lay at their feet.

"Gage." As if needing assurance that he was really there, she patted his shoulders and upper arms with shaking hands. She leaned her forehead against his chest. "Oh, God. It's you."

"Was it something I said?" he asked, aware that his heart was beating much faster than normal.

Kelsey laughed weakly, her fingers curling into his shirt, clinging for dear life. "I thought you were someone else."

"Anyone in particular? I know I've been out of the country for a few months but I wouldn't have thought it was long enough for manners to have changed that much. Is it customary to greet guests with a baseball bat now?"

She laughed again, the sound holding a hint of relieved tears. "I thought you were an ax murderer," she admitted with a watery chuckle.

Gage paused to absorb that. When he spoke again, there was an edge of steel in his voice. "And you figured you'd provide me with a bat to use for practice?" he asked in a deceptively gentle voice.

Kelsey winced. "I know it was stupid. But I woke up and heard a noise. And I thought it was probably a raccoon outside or a skunk."

"And you were going to bludgeon it into submission?" He nudged the bat with the side of his foot.

"I don't know what I was going to do," she admitted.

"You should have called 911."

"I know. But I thought it was probably nothing and I'd have felt like an idiot if the police came out and found nothing worse than a marauding skunk."

"Much better if they came out and found a crazed killer," Gage said, nodding his understanding.

"Okay, okay. So I was dumb." Kelsey was too relieved that it had been him to get seriously annoyed at his sarcasm. Besides, he was right. She should have called the police. "I'm glad it was you."

"So am I." Gage's arm tightened around her as he felt a shiver work its way up her spine. He pressed his cheek against her silky hair. He was still feeling a little shaky himself. First he'd found himself fending off a baseball bat and then he'd found out that Kelsey could have gotten herself killed if he really *had* been an intruder. If anything happened to Kelsey...

She shifted a little, and he was suddenly aware of the soft curves of her pressed against him, of the warm female body he was holding. Her knee-length cotton nightgown was perfectly modest, but he could feel the warmth of her skin through the fabric. Her hair was smooth as silk and held the faint floral scent of her shampoo. She felt quintessentially feminine, all curves and softness to complement the harder angles of his body.

Kelsey felt Gage's hold on her shift, his hand flattening against the middle of her back. She could feel the imprint of each finger on her skin and suddenly realized what flimsy protection her nightgown offered. Not that she needed protection from Gage, of course, but there was something startlingly intimate about the feel of his hand almost touching her skin. She could feel the steady beat of his heart under her cheek, the solid strength of muscles under her hands, pressed against the length of her body. She breathed in the faint scent of some woodsy after-shave and the warm, underlying scent of male underneath it. The scent made her want to snuggle closer, to breathe more deeply of the rich masculine scents, to feel—

Kelsey broke the thought off, feeling a blush work its way from her toes all the way to the top of her head until her entire body felt warmed by it. Good grief, what was wrong with her?

Gage suddenly became aware of the direction his thoughts were turning. Good God, what was he doing? This was Kelsey he was holding. His friend. Rick's wife.

It would have been impossible to say which of them moved first. At the same moment that Kelsey started to push herself away from him, Gage was releasing her as abruptly as if she'd suddenly caught fire. They stared at each other for a few seconds, tension humming between them—a tension to which neither was willing to put a name.

"You're home early," Kelsey said, breaking the silence before it could become uncomfortable.

"Actually I'm late." Gage ran his fingers through his hair, trying not to notice the subtle way her nightgown hinted at the curves of her slender body. Must be jet lag, he told himself. "I told Danny I'd be here Tuesday night. It's Wednesday morning," he pointed out, nodding to the clock. "I'd have been here hours ago, but the flight was delayed."

"He told me you said Thursday. He still gets mixed up on the days of the week." Kelsey's laugh was a little forced. She was suddenly feeling underdressed, which was ridiculous, considering her nightie was about as provocative as a nun's habit. Besides, this was Gage, for heaven's sake! She suddenly remembered the blow she'd aimed at him with the baseball bat. "Did I hurt you?"

"I'll live." Gage flexed his arm, thankful that his reflexes had been fast enough to block her jab. If she'd hit him in the stomach, he'd probably still be writhing in agony.

"I'm sorry. I thought you were—"

"An ax murderer," he finished for her. He had to repress a shudder when he considered what could have happened to her if he *had* been an intruder.

"I've got some ham leftover from Christmas dinner," Kelsey said, sensing the direction of his thoughts and deeming it prudent to offer a distraction. "And chocolate cake."

"Do you feed all the ax murderers you come across?" Gage asked.

"Only the ones I've known for years." She combed her fingers through her hair, trying to create some order in the tumbled mass. "Let me do something with my hair and I'll get you something to eat."

Gage watched her leave, his eyes unwillingly drawn to the sway of her hips.

"Jet lag," he muttered, hoping that's all it was.

Chapter 4

Gage's visit would be brief this time around, he told Kelsey over ham sandwiches and chocolate cake. He only had a week. They were shorthanded on the job, and it hadn't been easy to get even that much time off, but he'd wanted to spend at least part of the holiday with his family.

Kelsey was an only child, born fairly late in her parents' lives. Though she loved them dearly and knew the feeling was mutual, she couldn't really say that they were particularly close. Forty years had simply proved to be too wide a gap for them to bridge and develop a deep understanding of one another.

That lack made her all the more intrigued by the close ties that linked Gage to his family. The four brothers shared a bond she envied. Though she'd met all of the Walker men, Cole was the only one she knew more than superficially. Rick had known them better, having attended high school with Gage and spent time at his home while they were growing up. Rick had also been an only child but he hadn't shared Kelsey's wistful envy about having siblings.

"Are you kidding? Being an only child means you get all the attention. Who'd be dumb enough to want to share that?"

She smiled, remembering his exaggerated look of incredulity.

"You're smiling at your cake," Gage pointed out in a carefully neutral tone.

"Sorry." She glanced across the table at him, her gray eyes warm with remembered laughter. "I was just thinking about Rick's theory that being an only child was great because it meant that you got all the attention."

"I remember him pointing that out to me a time or two," Gage said, grinning. "I think he was hinting that I might want to dispose of a couple of excess siblings."

Kelsey laughed. "Could be. I always wanted a sister to share things with. Or that fabled big brother, the one who'd stand up for me and who also brought around a lot of cute friends."

"I've got two older brothers, and they were as likely to stand *on* me as they were to stand up for me. And they tended to be pretty possessive of any cute friends they had."

"I think the situation might have been different if you'd been a girl," Kelsey pointed out repressively.

"Maybe." Gage appeared to consider the possibility while he polished off his cake. "Maybe they wouldn't have stood on me quite so much if I'd been a girl," he conceded finally.

Kelsey laughed. "You're an idiot."

"Thank you."

A companionable silence fell between them, the kind possible only between two people who are completely comfortable with each other.

"How are you, Kelsey?"

Gage's question brought Kelsey's eyes across the table to meet his. The concern she saw there made her eyes sting. She blinked the feeling away and smiled at him.

"You mean, aside from fending off would-be ax murderers in the middle of the night?" She was pleased with the lightness of her tone, even more pleased to see his mouth quirk in a half smile.

"Aside from that," he agreed.

"I'm fine. Really," she added when he looked doubtful.

"You wouldn't lie to me, would you?" His tone was light but his eyes were searching.

"Yes, but I don't have to." Kelsey reached across the table to touch her fingertips to the back of his hand. Gage turned his hand palm up, catching her fingers in his. He stared down at their joined hands.

"It's been almost three years." He was speaking to himself as much as to her. She didn't have to ask what he was talking about. Rick was always with them.

"Sometimes it seems like twenty and sometimes it seems like just yesterday," Kelsey said softly. "I still miss him but I've gotten on with my life. I really am okay."

She met his searching look openly. There was nothing to hide. She'd made her peace with the empty place in her heart. Rick was gone but life moved on, and she'd had to make the choice to move with it or die with him. She'd made the only choice possible, thanks, in no small part, to the man sitting across the table from her.

"Good." Whatever Gage saw in her eyes must have convinced him that she really was doing all right. His fingers tightened over hers in a quick, affectionate squeeze before releasing her. "I'll help you clean up," he said, picking up his plate as he stood.

They cleared the table and loaded the dishwasher in companionable silence. The odd tension that had sprung up between them earlier was forgotten, nothing more than a shadow borne out of darkness and adrenaline.

Saturday mornings Kelsey left the house at the crack of dawn and drove to Santa Barbara to participate in the farmers' market there. The Saturday before New Year's Eve was no different. Her sales at the farmers' market were a vital part of her income. Besides, she liked the hustle and bustle, the chance to talk to other growers and exchange information with them.

Ordinarily she took Danny to her in-laws on Friday night and picked him up Saturday afternoon. Rick's parents welcomed the chance to spend time with their only grandchild, and Kelsey didn't have to find a way to entertain her son and handle customers at the same time. But Bill and Marilyn Jackson had left the day after Christmas for a two-week cruise, and Kelsey hadn't been able to find a replacement baby-sitter, which meant she had to take Danny to the market with her.

She wasn't looking forward to it. No matter how many toys and games she brought, he was bound to get bored long before it was time to come home, which was why she had to restrain the urge to fall on Gage's neck with gratitude when he offered to come with her and look after the booth and/or Danny.

"You don't have to do that," she said, trying not to look too pathetically eager.

She was sitting on the front porch, watching Gage and Danny play a game of catch. Since Danny's throwing skills were still somewhat marginal, it was more a game of fetch, with Gage spending most of his time chasing down a recalcitrant ball.

The temperature hovered in the low seventies, and the walkway was lined with the cheerful faces of the pansies she'd set out in the fall. It was hard to imagine that a good part of the country was dealing with ice and snow and thinking longingly of spring.

"I'll be there the whole morning, unless I sell out earlier," Kelsey warned.

"We can keep out of trouble that long, can't we, buddy?" he asked Danny.

"Sure, Uncle Gage," he agreed, his blue eyes bright with pleasure at being consulted.

"It's a lot to ask," Kelsey said, thinking she shouldn't take him up on his offer. "You've only got a few days home. It seems a shame for you to spend tomorrow stuck at a farmers' market, communing with vegetables and fruits."

"Sounds good to me. We like vegetables and fruits, don't we?"

"Sure." Danny's agreement was a little less definite on this score.

"I don't know." Kelsey eyed the two of them doubtfully. "It seems like a lot to ask."

"You're right." Gage lunged to catch a wild throw before looking at Kelsey. "It's an enormous amount to ask. I can't believe anyone would ask such a sacrifice. Fortunately for you, I volunteered."

"Did anyone ever tell you that sarcasm is unbecoming?"

Gage gave the question some thought, his dark brows coming together in a frown. He shook his head. "No. I don't think so. I've always thought it one of my better traits, actually."

Danny spoke before Kelsey could decide whether to laugh or throw something at Gage.

"We'll be good, Mama," he assured her, moving to stand at the foot of the porch steps and look up at her, his eyes pleading. "We won't be any trouble, will we, Uncle Gage?" He tilted his head back to look at Gage, his expression earnest.

"We'll be very good boys," Gage confirmed, reaching down to ruffle the boy's hair. He grinned at Kelsey, and it struck her that she'd never seen anyone who looked less like a good boy than Gage Walker. Not only was he most definitely a man but he was too wickedly attractive to look like anything but trouble.

He was wearing faded jeans that clung lovingly to his long legs and a black T-shirt with Donald Duck emblazoned across the front. The T-shirt was courtesy of Danny's last visit to Disneyland. He'd insisted that the T-shirt was the perfect Christmas gift for Uncle Gage. It should have looked a little silly on him, but instead of laughing at the cranky cartoon character, Kelsey found herself noticing the corded muscles in Gage's arms and the way the black fabric emphasized his golden tan. She wondered if he spent a lot of time working outside without a shirt, if his torso was as tanned as his arms.

For no particular reason, she found herself remembering how it had felt to be held against him, her breasts pressed to his chest, her hands wrapped around the hard muscles of his arms.

"Kelsey?" Gage's questioning tone and the quizzical tilt of his eyebrows snapped Kelsey out of her preoccupation. "Something wrong?"

She blinked, dragging her eyes from the width of his chest to his face. He was looking at her, his blue eyes holding both humor and a trace of concern.

"N-nothing's wrong." She had to clear her throat before she could get the assurance out. Hopefully the shadows on the porch were deep enough to conceal the fact that her face was almost hot enough to glow in the dark.

"I thought you'd gone into a trance there for a minute."

"I...ah...was just wondering if I should pull a few more baby carrots. Baby vegetables are one of my best sellers at the market." Not bad, as recoveries went, she congratulated herself. Now, if the fire in her face would just go out, she'd be doing pretty well.

"We thought maybe the idea of turning the two of us loose amongst all those vegetables had scared you so bad you couldn't talk, didn't we, buddy?"

"Yep." Danny leaned against Gage's leg and gazed up at him adoringly.

"You know, if you're going to keep an eye on Danny, there's no reason why the two of you have to come to the market with me. You could go off and do something else."

But Gage was already shaking his head. "We'll have more fun going with you. Right?"

Danny nodded, though he looked a little doubtful. Vegetables, on his plate or otherwise, were not exactly something he associated with fun. But if Gage thought it would be fun, he was clearly willing to give it a try.

"Consider it settled," Gage said. "You've got yourself a kid-sitter. Your troubles are at an end."

Not exactly, Kelsey thought, uneasily aware of the way the muscles in his arm rippled as he bent to scoop her son up under one arm and carry the giggling boy across the yard as if he were a football.

"I was starting to think I was going to have to conk him on the head to get him to go to sleep," Kelsey said as she entered the living room.

"He's an android," Gage moaned without lifting his head. He was lying on the sofa, which hadn't been designed to hold six feet two inches of prone male, with the result that, with his head pillowed on one end, his feet dangled off the other.

"It's obvious he's not human," he continued darkly. "A normal human being would have collapsed long before this."

"He's not an android, he's a four-year-old. They're related species, but not identical," Kelsey said. "They tend to be energetic."

"Energetic?" He raised his eyebrows in disbelief. "What I saw today goes way beyond such a simple explanation. That kind of energy has to come from an unnatural source, and I suspect it's got something to do with nuclear fusion."

"It's your own fault for suggesting that we go to the beach after the market closed."

"I was trying to be nice," Gage said indignantly. "I thought he'd enjoy the beach."

"He did."

"How could he enjoy it? He didn't stop moving long enough to look at it."

"Four-year-olds tend to approach life as participants rather than observers," Kelsey pointed out. "Besides, you didn't have to match him step for step. You could have sat on the beach and let him run off some of his energy."

"I was afraid he'd head for Catalina if I wasn't there to stop him."

"He can't swim that far yet."

"Who said anything about swimming? At the speeds he can attain, he could be across the channel without touching the water."

Kelsey laughed at Gage's aggrieved expression. He'd pushed the throw pillows off the sofa onto the floor, and she bent to pick one up. "Tuck this under your neck before it cracks," she told him.

"Why shouldn't it be like the rest of my body?" Gage asked. But he lifted his head and tucked the pillow under his neck.

"If the beach was so exhausting, why did you suggest following it up with hamburgers and a movie?"

"I'm his godfather. What else could I do?" he asked with a sigh that indicated great personal sacrifice.

"You were having as much fun as Danny. You just don't want to admit it," Kelsey told him briskly. "You'll live."

"I'm glad one of us is sure of that. Personally I have my doubts." He closed his eyes, the very picture of suffering. When Kelsey only laughed, Gage opened one eye to glare at her. "You're a heartless wretch. I was doing *you* a favor."

"I warned you that looking after a four-year-old wasn't easy," she reminded him.

"If you'd told me he was jet-propelled, I might have listened," he muttered.

"Do you think a cup of coffee would revive you?" she said, taking pity on him.

"Can I have a straw?" he asked weakly.

Kelsey was still smiling as she measured coffee into the coffeemaker. Gage made her smile more than anyone else she knew. The world always seemed a little brighter, life a little more interesting, when he was home.

She didn't know what she'd have done without him these past couple of years. Despite the fact that he was usually thousands of miles away, she'd always known he was there for her, a rock to lean on, something solid to cling to. Maybe it was a good thing he *had* been far away, she thought as she got out cups and a plate for cookies. If he'd been more available, she might not have been able to resist the urge to cling to him like a child. As it was, she'd learned to stand alone but she'd always known he was there to catch her if she fell. She and Danny were lucky to have him for a friend.

When she carried the tray of coffee and cookies into the living room a few minutes later, Gage was crouched by the fireplace, feeding kindling into the small fire he'd started. He turned to look at her, and for a moment the shadows made him almost a stranger. Kelsey felt her heart bump with a sudden, uneasy awareness of him as a man. He stood and then bent to lean the poker against the fireplace wall. She found herself noticing the way the faded denim of his jeans molded the long muscles of his thighs and cupped his buttocks.

"You're better than a St. Bernard and a keg of brandy." Gage grinned as he stepped forward to take the tray from her.

"Thanks. I think." Kelsey shook off her strange awareness and frowned at him. "I don't think I've ever been compared to a St. Bernard before. And so favorably, too. I'm flattered."

"I've never seen a St. Bernard who could bake." Gage set the tray on the coffee table in front of the sofa and reached for an oatmeal cookie even before he sat down.

"You're as bad as Danny," she said, sinking down on the sofa and picking up her coffee cup. "Didn't your mother ever tell you that too much sugar will rot your teeth?"

"Yeah, but I never believed her." Gage polished off the cookie and took another one before picking up his coffee cup and leaning back against the sofa. "I figured she was lying because she wanted to eat all the cookies herself."

"Mothers never lie."

"Mine did," he insisted. "Not only did she tell us that cookies would rot our teeth, but she tried to make us believe that brussels sprouts were good for us."

"But you didn't believe her?"

"I think Cole did. He was too young to know better. But Sam and Keefe and I all realized it was a lie. We'd hide them in our pockets and then bury them in the yard after supper."

"Your mother must have loved doing the laundry," Kelsey said with a shudder of sympathy. "Didn't

it occur to you that she might wonder what you'd had
in your pockets?''

"Nah." Gage leaned forward to pick up another
cookie. "But I remember being scared to death that
the brussels sprouts would live up to their name and
start growing and Mom would want to know how
they'd gotten into her rose beds.''

Kelsey laughed, picturing him as a boy stuffing unwanted vegetables in his pockets.

"The four of you must have made your mother's
life a living hell.''

"We did our best," he said with modest pride.

The conversation moved on to other things—Gage's
job, Kelsey's plans for expanding her business. She
had read about some techniques for increasing pro-
ductivity that she was eager to try out when she put in
her spring and summer crops. She also hoped to put
in a greenhouse in a year or two, maybe experiment
with growing plants to sell.

Gage's stint in South America was almost over. He
wasn't sure where he'd be going when this job ended.
There was a project in Africa that sounded interesting....

"Don't you ever get tired of traveling?" Kelsey
leaned her head against the back of the sofa and gave
Gage a questioning look. "Don't you ever want to
settle down, stay home?''

Home? Gage considered the word in relationship to
himself and came up blank. Where was home? His
mother's house in Los Olivos? She'd say it was his
home. As far as Rachel Walker was concerned, her
house would always be a home to her sons. But it
wasn't *his* home, not anymore. It hadn't been since he
left for college. Since then, he'd lived in a lot of dif-

ferent places—dorm rooms, apartments, hotels, tents and huts—but none of them had been home.

In the past fifteen years, the closest thing he'd had to a home was right here. From the moment Rick and Kelsey bought this house, it had become almost as much his home as theirs. They'd made it his, opening it to him, acting as if there was nothing more natural than for him to stay with them whenever he was in the country, for him to treat their home as if it were also his.

Home? He didn't have one of his own, only this one that he borrowed from time to time, like someone putting on a rented costume and playing pretend for a little while. It was a bleak realization to think this was probably all he'd ever have of home.

"Gage?" Kelsey's questioning tone made Gage realize how much time had passed since she'd asked if he ever got tired of traveling.

"Hmm?" Pulling his gaze from the fire, he looked at her, his eyebrows raised in question as if he hadn't caught her words. "Sorry. I was thinking of something else. What did you say?"

"I asked if you ever get tired of traveling and think of maybe settling down."

"I never think about it," he lied. "I don't think I'm the hearth-and-home type. Wanderlust in the blood, maybe."

"You might change your mind if you fell in love with a homebody," Kelsey said, her tone lightly teasing.

"Maybe I'll just make it a point to fall in love with a gypsy," he said lightly.

"You'd have to find one first. They aren't exactly common these days, you know."

"A sad commentary on modern society," he said solemnly.

"A clear indication of decay run rampant," Kelsey agreed, shaking her head.

To Gage's relief, the conversation moved away from the likelihood of his settling down or getting married. He'd long ago made peace with the choices he'd made, but there was something about discussing them with Kelsey that made him aware of a loneliness he preferred not to acknowledge. Better by far to push it away, bury it deep inside and pretend it didn't exist.

It was almost midnight when Kelsey stood. "I'd better get to bed. Danny will be up at six."

"After the day he had, I would have thought he'd need more time to recuperate." Gage rose, too.

"Four-year-olds recharge pretty quickly."

"He's an android," he muttered as he bent to pick up the tray that held their coffee cups and the empty cookie plate. Her chuckle followed him from the room.

When he returned a few minutes later, Kelsey was just turning off the lamp on her way out of the living room. Over her shoulder, he could see that she'd closed the fireplace doors and straightened the cushions on the sofa.

"The dishwasher was full so I turned it on," he said, jerking his head in the direction of the kitchen, where the hum of the dishwasher could be heard.

"A man who can run a dishwasher. I'm impressed," Kelsey said with an exaggerated look of admiration.

"Don't be sexist," he ordered sternly. "This is the nineties, remember? Men are allowed to stretch to fill nontraditional roles."

"Gee, and I thought all they were good for is opening pickle jars." Kelsey fluttered her eyelashes in a fair imitation of helpless femininity.

Gage's glance went over her head, and his grin widened. "Now, there's an invitation I can't resist."

"What?" Kelsey's brows rose questioningly.

"That."

She followed his gaze, tilting her head back to stare at the dusty little bundle of foliage thumbtacked to the doorjamb over her head. It took her a moment to realize what it was. Mistletoe.

"Who put...Susan must have hung it," she said, answering her own half-spoken question.

"Susan?"

"Danny's baby-sitter. She's seventeen and a firm believer in tradition. Which I've always thought was interesting, considering she had her belly button pierced last summer, and since then has been trying to decide whether a nose ring would be the perfect finishing touch or a bit of overkill."

"A tough decision," Gage said, looking less than solemn.

"It is when you're seventeen and torn between entering a convent and pursuing your dream of playing guitar in a heavy-metal band."

"You're kidding, right?" Gage's expression hovered between laughter and disbelief.

"Scout's honor." Kelsey held up one hand in the appropriate gesture.

"Maybe she could combine the two, update the image of the singing nun," he suggested.

Kelsey shook her head. "I know they've loosened the rules up a bit but I think the Vatican probably draws the line at nose rings."

"Very narrow of them," Gage said, shaking his head sadly.

"I'm sure Susan would agree with you."

"Well, nose ring or no, we can't let her down," Gage said, nodding to the mistletoe.

"I won't tell her if you don't."

"It's seven years' bad luck to ignore mistletoe," he said, slipping one arm around her waist.

"I think that's if you break a mirror." Kelsey's voice was suddenly breathless.

Gage felt a little breathless himself. He'd forgotten how small she was. She was so full of energy and determination that it was easy to forget what a delicate package that energy came in. It was only now, holding her in his arms, that he was reminded of her fragility, of the warm feminine curves of her.

The light from the hall shone over his shoulder, illuminating her face. Her mouth was still curved with laughter, but there was a flicker of uncertainty in her eyes, an uneasiness that Gage chose to ignore.

"I'm sure Susan didn't expect anyone to actually pay any attention to that thing," Kelsey said, staring up at him with wide gray eyes.

"Then, traditionalist that she is, she'll be pleased to know we put it to use, after all." *Don't do it, Walker,* a voice whispered inside as his head dipped toward hers. *You're going to regret this.*

But not half as much as he would if he stopped now.

"Susan's no botanical genius," Kelsey muttered. "It's probably not even mistletoe."

"It's the thought that counts," Gage murmured, and set his mouth to hers.

Bad idea. The words echoed in his head. He'd intended nothing more than a gentle kiss, a gesture of affection between friends. And maybe that's all it would have been if her mouth hadn't yielded so sweetly beneath his.

He felt her breath catch, felt his own heart still for an instant before starting again, the rhythm much too quick and hard. There was a moment when time stood still, when he could have stepped back, defused the danger with a grin and a light comment, when everything could have gone on just as it always had.

An instant only, and then everything changed. It happened so quickly—the shift from laughter to need, from smiles to passion. There was no gentle transition, no gradual slide from one stage to the next. It all changed in a heartbeat.

Did his arms tighten around her, or did she press closer to him? Did he ask admittance into the warmth of her mouth, or did her lips part to invite him inside? It didn't matter. Nothing mattered but the taste of her, the feel of her body against his.

It was like being in the midst of a raging inferno—all heat and sound. Blinded by the heat, Gage buried his hand in the heavy gold of Kelsey's hair, tilting her head back to allow him better access to her mouth. His tongue slid inside, demanding and receiving her complete response.

The low whimper in her throat might have been protest if her fingers hadn't been buried in his hair, if her body hadn't been arched to his.

God, it had been so long. His mouth devoured hers. He was starving for the taste of her, the feel of her. He'd hungered for so long, wanted for so many years. She was everything he'd thought she would be. Her body fit against his as if designed to be there, as if meant for him alone. She was so right in his arms. So very, very right.

Kelsey curled her fingers deeper into the thick blackness of Gage's hair, pressed herself closer to the warmth of him. He tasted of coffee and oatmeal cookies—an impossibly erotic combination. He smelled of wood smoke, cologne and man. He was all muscle and heat.

She wanted to curl deeper into his arms, lose herself in the heat of him. It felt so good to be held, to be kissed, not to be alone anymore. She'd been cold and alone for so long, so terribly long.

Gage's hand slid under the hem of her sweatshirt, his fingers splaying against the small of her back. His touch burned to the core of her, starting a deep, throbbing pulse in the pit of her stomach, a hunger so powerful it frightened Kelsey into some sense of what she was doing.

Wrong.

The thought beat sluggishly in her brain. No matter how right it felt, it couldn't be. Couldn't be. This was wrong.

Wrong.

Gage tried to push the thought away, but it refused to go. This was wrong. *Kelsey is Rick's wife. Your best friend's wife. What are you doing? She's another man's wife. Rick's wife. Rick's wife. Rick's wife.*

Kelsey's hands flattened against his chest just as Gage lifted his head. They stared at each other, smoky gray eyes meeting electric blue. Between them lay the rubble of what they'd thought their relationship to be—destroyed in the blazing force of that one kiss.

My God, what have I done? Gage stepped back from Kelsey, staggered by the sheer magnitude of the disaster looming before them. *She's Rick's wife—his wife, for God's sake.*

What was I thinking? Kelsey's hands jerked back from Gage's chest as if his shirt had just caught fire. *This was Gage. Her friend, Rick's best friend. Oh, God. Rick. What had she done?*

"Kelsey, I—"

"That was a surprise, wasn't it?" she interrupted in a tone of such false brightness that it made her teeth hurt.

She had to make this right, had to smooth it over. She could see the look in Gage's eyes, see the shock and guilt. He'd leave. He'd leave and never come back. She couldn't lose him. Not him, too. They could fix this. They could get past it. They had to, she thought frantically.

"A surprise?" Gage said slowly.

"I guess that must really be mistletoe."

"I guess so. Kelsey, I didn't—"

"Neither did I." She stopped and drew a quick breath. This time her smile was a little less forced. "Let's not blow this out of proportion, Gage."

"Out of proportion?" His arched brow made it clear that he thought that would be hard to do. "Kelsey, what just happened—"

"A kiss. That's all that happened. Things just got a little out of hand."

Gage looked as if he doubted her sanity, but Kelsey kept her expression perfectly calm. Or as calm as was possible when her skin tingled with awareness and her pulse was still double its normal rate, not to mention the fact that her knees were not quite steady.

"A little out of hand," Gage repeated slowly, as if trying to connect the trite phrase to what had just occurred between them.

"We're adults. We know better than to let something like this cause problems."

Please, Gage. Please don't let it cause problems. I need you in my life. In Danny's life. We can get past this. We can pretend it never happened. Please, Gage.

Maybe he read the plea in her eyes. Or maybe he realized that she was right, that the only way to deal with what had happened was to pretend there was nothing to deal with. Whatever the reason, he nodded slowly.

"No reason it should cause problems," he said quietly, his eyes shuttered. "It was just a kiss."

"That's right," Kelsey said, her voice too loud and too bright, almost echoing in the quiet house. "No big deal," she added for emphasis.

There was a brief silence, taut with things unsaid, unacknowledged. Kelsey had the sudden, frightening thought that she'd never be able to look at him again without remembering how it had felt to have him hold her, kiss her.

Mumbling something that could have been either "good night" or a stifled sob, she slipped past him and all but ran down the hall to her room.

Gage stayed where he was for what seemed like a very long time. Staring at the dying fire, he tried to sort out what had happened, how things had gotten out of hand. He glanced over his head at the dusty little sprig of leaves and berries. Reaching up, he tugged it loose, cupping it in his hand and studying it as if it could provide the answers he needed.

But the only thing that was clear was the fact that he'd kissed Kelsey the way he would have kissed a lover. Kelsey—Rick's wife, his friend. Kelsey, whom he'd promised himself—and Rick—he'd take care of.

She'd made it clear that she wanted to simply put the moment behind them, pretend nothing had happened. She was right. Anything else would make things untenable.

Gage walked over to the fireplace. Tugging open the door, he threw the sprig of mistletoe onto the bed of coals. For a moment, it lay there, untouched by the heat. Tendrils of smoke curled up around the edges of the leaves. The little red ribbon bow burst into flame first, followed an instant later by the mistletoe itself.

Gage stood watching until it burned to ashes, trying not to think about how good Kelsey had felt in his arms.

And how much he'd like to have her there again.

By morning Gage and Kelsey had virtually forgotten all about the kiss they'd shared under the mistletoe. Of course they had. Neither of them gave a thought to the heat they'd generated. Certainly not.

And neither of them thought it at all significant that Gage chose to drive to Los Angeles a day early just to be sure he wouldn't miss his plane. It was perfectly understandable that he'd rather spend the night on a sofa in his brother's studio apartment than sleep in his own bed in the room he rented from Kelsey. The most natural thing in the world.

And if there'd been any lingering thoughts about that incendiary kiss, they certainly had faded by the time Gage came home again. No one remembered something like that for six months. Perhaps there were one or two uneasy moments, a certain awareness, but that soon faded, and by the time Gage had left again, everything was back on its old footing. The whole incident was completely forgotten.

Really.

Chapter 5

"I wish you could come back with Danny, Kelsey."

Kelsey winced at the wistful tone of her mother's voice. "I wish I could, too, Mom, but this is a busy time of year for me. The gardens are in full swing, and I've got a lot of orders to fill. It's not like Minnesota, where you've still got a foot of snow on the ground."

"We do not!" Viola Sinclair never failed to rise to that particular bait. An avid gardener herself, she was openly envious of her daughter's year-round growing season. "We haven't had snow in weeks!"

"We haven't had snow in years," Kelsey teased. She shifted the phone from one ear to the other to ease the strain on her neck. It was a good thing they hadn't invented an affordable video phone yet, she thought as she sorted through a pile of laundry. Talking on the phone was some of the most productive time she had.

"Never mind about the snow," Vi said, refusing to

be sidetracked. "Have you given any thought to what your father and I suggested at Christmas?"

"That Danny and I move back to Minnesota?" Kelsey stared at the half-dozen child-size socks lying on the bed. How was it possible to have so many socks and have none of them match any of the others? What did Danny do with them? Trade them with friends at school so they could all drive their mothers crazy trying to find matched pairs?

"There's plenty of room here, and the schools are good. You wouldn't have to work so hard."

"I like my work, Mom."

"And you wouldn't have to worry about making ends meet."

"My ends are meeting pretty well these days." Kelsey dropped the unmatched socks into the dirty-clothes basket. Maybe if she ran them through the wash again, they'd miraculously turn up with mates.

"Your father and I rattle around in this big old house. You and Danny would have lots of room."

"We've got room here, Mom. This house is plenty big for the two of us." She rubbed two fingers over the ache building across the bridge of her nose. They'd had this same conversation half a dozen times since Christmas, and she got the same headache every time. She knew what was coming next, could almost have recited the dialogue.

"It's a cute little place but it's not really family-size, is it? I mean, there's really only room for you and Danny, isn't there?"

"Danny and I *are* a family, Mom," Kelsey said, trying not to sound impatient.

"I know you are," Vi said quickly. "I didn't mean to imply that you weren't. But if you were to get married again, there's no room for more children."

The ache became a throb that spread outward to encompass her entire forehead. Carrying the portable phone with her, Kelsey headed for the kitchen and the aspirin bottle. *She means well. She means well.* Kelsey recited the phrase like a mantra.

"I'm not even dating anyone. I think it's a little soon to be worrying about where our children will sleep."

The childproof lid on the aspirin bottle proved to be in a recalcitrant mood. Tucking the phone between her shoulder and her ear, she listened as her mother reminded her that she was still a young woman; Rick would never have wanted her to spend the rest of her life alone. It was time she started thinking about the future. Danny wouldn't be with her forever, you know.

"I've got another twelve years or so before I have to start worrying about an empty nest." Kelsey lined up the arrows, as instructed, and tried to pry the lid off with her thumb. It didn't budge.

"You probably think I'm sticking my nose in where it doesn't belong," Vi reflected.

"Actually I do think that," Kelsey said, driven to honesty by her throbbing head. "But I know it's because you love me," she added into the shocked silence.

"I just don't think you should mourn forever," Vi said, her voice a little stiff. "It's been over four years since Rick's death, you know. He'd want you to get on with your life."

"I know, Mom. It's not Rick's memory that keeps me from dating. It's that I'm just too busy to think about it. My life is full. I'm happy." *Except at moments like this.*

In desperation she banged the aspirin bottle on the edge of the sink. The lid popped off abruptly, shooting toward Kelsey's face. Startled, she jerked back. Aspirin flew from the open bottle, pattering onto the kitchen floor like fat white raindrops.

"I really don't mean to be a pushy mother but I worry about you."

"I know you do, Mom." Kelsey crouched down and began picking aspirin up off the floor. *Make a note, Kelsey. Don't ever tell Danny you're worried about him—the most guilt-provoking maternal line ever invented.* "You don't need to worry about me, though. Danny and I are doing just fine. We've both got lots of friends here. In fact, Clair Miller called a few days ago. She's living in Santa Barbara now and she's coming over for lunch later today."

"I thought Clair was married and living in Europe somewhere."

"She was." Kelsey breathed a silent sigh of relief that her mother had been distracted from her favorite topic. "But she's divorced now and she's decided to open a boutique in Santa Barbara. We've talked on the phone a few times, but this is our first chance to get together since she got home. In fact, I hate to cut this short but I've got a lot to do before she gets here."

It took her another twenty minutes to get her mother off the line. Vi couldn't hang up without mentioning—again—that there was plenty of room for her and Danny in her childhood home and, by the way, had she mentioned that Mrs. Armato's son had moved home? Hadn't Kelsey dated him in high school? He was a lawyer now and still handsome as sin.

Kelsey rolled her eyes. Kenny Armato might look like a Greek god, but she was willing to bet that he still had more hands than an octopus had tentacles. She murmured something noncommittal and carefully selected two relatively dust-free aspirins from the fistful she held. She put them in her mouth and washed them down with the cold remains of her morning cup of coffee while her mother expounded on the advantages of raising a child in a small town.

Kelsey could have pointed out that she wasn't exactly living in a booming metropolis, but it would have been a waste of breath. As far as Vi Sinclair was concerned, California—and most particularly *Southern* California—was one vast, sprawling, smog-bound city.

Her mother was finally starting to wind down when Gage walked into the kitchen. He caught the harried look in her eyes and paused on his way to the refrigerator. His gaze took in the phone caught between her chin and her shoulder, the empty aspirin bottle on the counter, the pile of aspirin next to it and the cold cup of coffee she clutched between her hands.

"Your mother?" he mouthed.

When Kelsey nodded, he gave her a look of such profound sympathy that Kelsey nearly choked trying to turn a laugh into a shallow cough. She sent him a stern glare and received an unrepentant grin in return.

Listening to her mother expound on the virtues of Kenny Armato and his law degree, Kelsey briefly considered mentioning that Gage was home for a few weeks. It would certainly change the subject but it would only lengthen the conversation. Vi Sinclair's second-favorite source of maternal concern—coming right after the fact that her daughter didn't seem interested in finding another husband—was the fact that Gage lived in that same daughter's house.

It wasn't that she had anything against Gage personally, she'd said repeatedly. He'd seemed perfectly nice when she met him at Rick and Kelsey's wedding, and she certainly appreciated that he'd been a great help to Kelsey since Rick's death. It was their living arrangements of which she disapproved. She didn't like the idea of her daughter's sharing her home with an attractive man, even if it was only for a few weeks out of every year.

This might be the nineties, but times hadn't changed that much, she'd said in a tone that brooked no argument. A man and a woman, alone in a house together—and never mind Danny, who was too young to count—well, there wasn't much question about where something like that was likely to lead, no matter how late in the century it happened to be.

Ridiculous, Kelsey thought. She and Gage were friends. No matter what her mother thought, it *was* possible for a man and a woman to have a platonic friendship. True, there'd been that one incident, she remembered uneasily. But that had been almost a year and a half ago. They'd put that behind them, dismissed it as nothing more than temporary insanity. Gage was her friend.

He opened the refrigerator door and took out a can of cola. He popped the aluminum tab and lifted the can to his mouth. He'd been working outside, clearing land for the greenhouse she'd bought—hot, thirsty labor. Kelsey watched his throat work as he swallowed.

Her eyes drifted from there to the corded muscles in his arms. He was wearing a ratty blue tank top, streaked with white from some long-ago laundry accident, torn in so many places that it should have been relegated to rag duty ages ago. The cotton knit, worn thin with age, clung lovingly to his muscled torso. With his arm lifted as he drank, the hem of the shirt rode up, revealing the taut flatness of his stomach and the silky dark hair that arrowed downward to disappear into the waistband of the faded cutoffs that rode scandalously low on his narrow hips.

Kelsey realized where her eyes, not to mention her imagination, were headed and turned abruptly away. Her fingers tightened painfully over the phone, her mother's voice a vague mutter in her ear. Her cheeks felt flushed, as if she'd been caught in some crime.

What on earth was the matter with her? Staring at Gage like that? As if he were . . . something other than a friend. As if he were a man. Which he was, of course. But she wasn't supposed to think of him that way. She *didn't* think of him that way.

Kelsey closed her eyes, struggling to get a firm grip on her spinning thoughts. It was really her mother's fault, she decided. With all her mother's talk about second marriages and urging her to get on with her life, she'd been thrown off-balance.

Relieved to have someone to blame for the disconcerting direction her thoughts had taken, Kelsey returned her attention to the voice on the other end of the line. Luckily her mother didn't require much help to keep a conversation flowing and she hadn't noticed anything lacking in Kelsey's occasional mutters of agreement. Kelsey reminded her mother that she had a guest coming for lunch, agreed to think about what the other woman had said—though which part she was supposed to consider, she hadn't the slightest idea—and promised to give Danny a kiss from his granny and grandad when he got home from school.

"The Minnesota-is-heaven-California-is-a-den-of-iniquity speech?" Gage asked as she pushed the antenna back into place and set the portable phone on the counter.

"Pretty much," Kelsey agreed. She turned to look at him and was relieved to find that her pulse stayed steady and her hormones didn't start doing handsprings. The smile she gave him was bright with relief. "Don't forget Clair is coming for lunch."

"Clair?" He gave her a blank look.

"Clair Miller. I mentioned it a couple of days ago."

"The girl you went to school with, right?" He closed his fist over the empty soda can, crushing it with easy strength before dropping it in the recycling bin under the sink.

"That's the one. You met her at the wedding. She was one of the bridesmaids. You sat with her at the reception."

Gage pulled another can of soda out of the refrigerator and turned to look at her. He was frowning slightly. "Does she have red hair?"

"She's a brunette. Or at least she was then. I haven't seen her in a few years, so it might have changed. Very pretty. Great figure."

Kelsey told herself that she wasn't pleased when Gage shrugged to indicate that the description didn't mean anything to him. Or, if she was just the tiniest bit pleased, it was simply because she'd played second fiddle to Clair all through high school and it was nice to know that there was one man at least who hadn't been bowled over by her looks.

"You'll recognize her when you see her," she told him, and then was ashamed of herself for hoping he didn't. "You're welcome to join us for lunch."

"Thanks, but if you haven't seen her in a while, I'm sure you two have a lot to talk about. I think I'll give Cole a call and see if he wants to grab a burger somewhere."

"You don't have to leave," Kelsey said.

"I know but I've been home two weeks and I've barely said hello to the family. I might as well start with Cole."

"You've been working so hard on the greenhouse that you haven't had time to see your family." Kelsey was immediately guilt stricken. When she'd told him that she'd found a great bargain on a used greenhouse, he pushed her to buy it, offering the incentive of his cheap labor to put it up. That had made all the difference to her budget, and she'd solidified the deal immediately. He'd been working on the site ever since.

"You're working too hard," she said, sounding as guilty as she felt. "You're on vacation. You should be relaxing, not working on my greenhouse."

"Yeah, you're a regular slave driver, all right. Maybe you should give me a little more gruel to keep up my strength." He popped the top on the second can of cola and gave her a dry look. "I could point out that you didn't exactly shanghai me into this job, I volunteered."

"But it's your vacation, and you're working like a dog."

"Now, there's a phrase I've never understood," Gage said, pausing with the bright red can halfway to his mouth." 'Working like a dog.' What exactly does that mean? Personally most of the dogs I've known don't do a whole lot of work. My mother's dog, for example, has never done a day's work in his life."

"Is this the dog who stole the Thanksgiving turkey last year? Moose or something?"

"Hippo," Gage corrected her. He grinned, remembering the chaos that had followed the dog's theft of the main course. "He's the one. But I was thinking of honest work, not burglary. Name me one dog who really works."

"Lassie," Kelsey said promptly.

"She's got stunt doubles." Gage shook his head, dismissing Lassie out of hand. "And did you know she's a he?" He shook his head. "All those years I watched that show and never realized Lassie was a cross dresser."

"A cross dresser?" Kelsey had just pulled two heads of lettuce out of the refrigerator and was reaching for the bundle of baby carrots she'd pulled hours before, but at Gage's comment she forgot the carrots and turned to look at him. "You're calling Lassie a cross dresser?"

"Hey, I didn't mean it as an insult." He waved the cola can in an expansive gesture. "I'm a firm supporter of alternative life-styles."

"We're talking about a dog, Gage."

"Yeah?" He gave her a blank look. "So what's your point?"

It occurred to her that he'd very neatly turned the conversation away from the topic of his working on the greenhouse. After this ridiculous exchange, there was no way she could attempt any serious discussion, not while her mind was still reeling with the concept of Lassie's being a cross dresser. And he knew it, darn him.

She debated throwing the lettuce at his head and then decided it would do no good. It wouldn't help restore a more serious tone to the conversation and would just bruise a perfectly good head of Black Seeded Simpson, which happened to be her favorite lettuce.

"You have a really sick sense of humor, Walker."

"Thank you." He looked so genuinely pleased that Kelsey couldn't hold back a laugh.

One of the things she missed most when Gage was gone was the way he made her laugh. It wasn't that she didn't laugh at other times. She just seemed to do more of it when he was around.

"I think you're exaggerating." Kelsey sent a look of laughing accusation across the table. Clair widened her eyes innocently.

"Scout's honor, Kels. He really did expect me to say good-night to every portrait every night. We'd walk the length of the whole bloody portrait gallery with him saying good-night to every DiMera who'd ever lived. And they were a ridiculously prolific family. It took *hours*."

"If he was such a nut case, why did you marry him?"

"I didn't know." Clair tapped the ash off her cigarette into a clay pot base, the closest thing to an ashtray Kelsey had been able to come up with. They'd moved their lunch outside so that Clair could smoke, which she'd done nonstop since her arrival almost an hour ago.

"He seemed pretty normal when we met," she continued, waving the cigarette for emphasis. "Good-looking, if you could ignore the weak chin, and charming as hell. He actually kissed my hand when we were introduced. What girl wouldn't marry a guy who'd kiss her hand?"

"It would be hard to resist."

"Okay, so you would have resisted." Clair was not fooled in the least by Kelsey's solemn tone. "You always did have more sense than I did, especially when it came to men."

"I just wanted different things." Kelsey nibbled a shred of carrot that had been left on the edge of her plate. "I wanted a home and a family."

"And I wanted to be rich and see the world." Clair's mouth twisted in a rueful smile. "Isn't there some annoying cliché about being careful what you wish for because you may get it? I figure that Carlos turning out to be a fruitcake is my punishment for having such a shallow wish. If I'd wanted something a little more mature, like you did, maybe I wouldn't have been so dazzled by an Italian suit and an accent."

"Things didn't work out exactly the way I'd planned, either," Kelsey said quietly, thinking of Rick.

"I know they didn't, honey. I didn't mean to imply that you'd had life easy." Clair reached across the picnic table to touch the back of Kelsey's hand in a quick gesture of apology.

"I didn't think you did." Which was nothing less than the truth. She'd never had any trouble seeing through the sharp-tongued persona Clair liked to project.

"I know how much you loved Rick. I'm not comparing losing him to my divorce from Carlos."

"A divorce isn't an easy thing."

"It wasn't that bad." Clair stubbed out her cigarette and immediately reached for the pack to light another one. Her quick, nervous movements were at odds with her throwaway tone. "After two years of living in that drafty mausoleum, it was a pleasure to get back to the States where central heating is an inalienable right."

"That's a part of the constitution I don't remember," Kelsey said with a grin.

"Trust me, it's right up there with life, liberty and the right to arm bears."

Kelsey choked on her iced tea. "I think that's the 'right to bear arms,'" she corrected when she'd regained her breath.

"Bear arms, arm bears." Clair waved her cigarette in a gesture of indifference. "What difference does it make?"

"I'd guess it makes a lot of difference to hikers. They'd probably get a little nervous if they thought the local bears were packing Uzis."

"I can see how that might be a problem. The bears wouldn't have to raid the garbage anymore. They could just take what they wanted at gunpoint."

"Your honey or your life."

The two of them dissolved into giggles.

"I've missed you," Clair said when their laughter had subsided.

"I've missed you, too. I'm glad you're settling close enough that we'll be able to see each other." Kelsey stood and began clearing the remains of their lunch from the table.

"That was one of the reasons I picked Santa Barbara, because you were in the area." Clair rose and stubbed out her half-smoked cigarette before picking up her plate and the big salad bowl. "So far, we've done nothing but talk about me. Now I want to hear all the gory details of what's going on in your life."

"There's not much to tell. Running the business and raising Danny pretty much fill my life. No time for Italian counts with weak chins and lots of ancestors," she added, slanting a teasing glance in Clair's direction.

"You haven't missed anything there." Clair hooked one finger around the screen door handle and pulled it open, stepping back to allow Kelsey to go through first. "I thought the hunk from the wedding was living with you," she said as they entered the kitchen. "That's better than an Italian count any day."

"The hunk from the wedding?" Kelsey set the plates on the counter and turned to take the salad bowl from Clair. "You mean Gage Walker?"

"Tall, dark, chiseled jaw, electric blue eyes, body to die for? That's the one."

Kelsey's smile felt a little forced. Clair's description of Gage was accurate enough. It was just that she didn't think of him in those terms.

"Tall, dark and handsome," Clair continued, oblivious to Kelsey's silence. "I've never seen anyone make a cliché look quite so good."

"He is an attractive man," Kelsey said, aware that the description was a little bland. Apparently Clair agreed.

"*Attractive?*" She gave her friend a look of disbelief. "You've been spending too much time communing with zucchini. Unless he's aged really badly since the wedding, Gage Walker is considerably more than just 'attractive.' The man is a major hunk.''

"Hmm." Kelsey turned the water on harder than necessary and began to rinse the dishes. She'd almost forgotten some of Clair's more annoying tendencies.

"He is still living here, isn't he?" Clair asked, raising her voice to be heard over the sound of the water.

"When he's not out of the country," Kelsey said. She clattered the plates together deliberately, hoping the noise would discourage conversation. She should have known better. Clair simply talked louder.

"Well?"

"Well what?"

"What's going on?"

"I don't know what you mean." There were no more dishes to rinse. It was a shame she hadn't made a more elaborate meal, Kelsey thought, looking around for a forgotten fork. But there was nothing, and she reluctantly shut the water off and turned to look at her friend.

Clair was sitting at the kitchen table, her long, slender legs crossed at the knee. In her trim, camel-colored slacks and jade silk camp shirt, she looked elegantly casual, as if she were about to pose for a spread in some upscale fashion magazine. Her dark hair was cut short, forming a sleek cap that framed her face, and emphasized her high cheekbones and the faintly exotic slant of her dark eyes.

"I mean, what's going on between you and Gage Walker," Clair said, speaking slowly and distinctly and leaving no room for evasion.

"We're friends." Kelsey finished drying her hands on a red-and-white-checked towel and tossed it on the counter.

"Just friends?" Clair arched one perfectly shaped brow, as if she found Kelsey's description hard to believe.

"It is possible for a man and a woman to be friends," Kelsey said, aware that she sounded a little defensive.

"Sure it is. I just can't imagine being friends with someone that gorgeous. It's tough to be friends with someone when all you can think about is what he'd be like in bed."

"I don't think of Gage that way," Kelsey said primly.

"The two of you have never..." Clair let the question trail off, raising her brows again, her dark eyes full of curiosity.

"Never." She shoved aside the memory of Gage's holding her, kissing her.

"Then you wouldn't object to me trying my hand with him?" Clair asked.

"Of course not." Kelsey forced a laugh, wondering why she'd never realized just how predatory Clair could look.

"It just seems a shame to leave such a gorgeous guy laying around unclaimed."

"You make him sound like a package in the dead letter office. I don't think Gage is pining for female companionship."

"He's dating someone?"

"Not that I know of." But she wasn't as sure as she sounded. It suddenly occurred to Kelsey that she didn't really know whether or not Gage was dating someone. She'd never even considered the possibility. Now that she thought about it, why *wouldn't* he be dating?

And why should the idea bother her?

"Then it can't hurt to throw myself at him, can it?" Clair's question was a welcome distraction. "If you're sure you don't mind?"

Kelsey knew she should appreciate Clair's concern for her feelings. She knew she should wish her luck with Gage. She liked Clair. She liked Gage. Why shouldn't she like the two of them together? The only answer that came to mind was one more suited to her six-year-old son—*just 'cause.*

"Of course I don't mind," she said, forcing a smile that felt as phony as the words tasted. "He was going to pick Danny up from school so he should be home before too long, if you wanted to stay until he gets here."

"Seems to be a day for renewing old acquaintances, doesn't it?" Clair said, giving Kelsey a warm smile.

"Yes." Kelsey returned the smile, wishing she could feel a little more enthused.

She and Clair had been best friends all through high school and college. Even after their marriages had put thousands of miles between them, they'd kept in touch. She'd been genuinely pleased to learn that Clair was moving to Santa Barbara and had looked forward to renewing their friendship. She still was. Really.

"I've got strawberries for dessert," she said, moving to the refrigerator.

It wasn't that she wasn't glad to see Clair. It was just that, next to Clair's sleek sophistication, she felt old and frumpy. The khaki trousers and short-sleeved cotton shirt that had looked crisp and summery when she put them on suddenly seemed dull and boring.

Maybe she should get a haircut, she thought as she set the bowl of strawberries on the counter. She'd kept her hair a little more than shoulder length because it was easy to take care of and she could pull it up into a ponytail and get it out of her way when she was working in the gardens. But maybe she should think about a new cut—something short and sassy.

She spooned the sliced berries into two small bowls. And maybe she should start spending a little more time on her makeup. A dash of mascara and a dusting of blush wasn't exactly making the most of herself. Yes, she was busy but not so busy that she couldn't spend a few more minutes on her appearance each day.

"These look delicious," Clair said as Kelsey set the bowls on the table. "It's too bad Carlos isn't here."

"Your ex-husband?" Kelsey gave her a surprised look. "I thought you were glad to be rid of him. Why is it too bad he's not here?"

"He's violently allergic to strawberries," Clair said with a wicked grin.

Kelsey laughed with her, feeling a twinge of shame at the direction her thoughts had taken. What was wrong with her? You'd think they were back in high school, competing for the same boy. She must have spent too much time in the sun.

If Clair wanted to go out with Gage, she certainly had no objections. Good grief, it wasn't as if she had any claim on him herself. Or wanted one, for that matter.

Chapter 6

She was *not* waiting up for him.

There were any number of perfectly valid reasons for her to be lying awake at—Kelsey glanced at the clock—twelve-fifteen in the morning. Not one of them had anything to do with the fact that Gage had taken Clair out to dinner and a movie.

She stared at the bedroom ceiling and enumerated some of those reasons. She'd had a busy week and was too tired to sleep. She was worried about the cabbage moths she'd seen fluttering around the broccoli this afternoon. And there was the problem of what would be ready to take to market Saturday morning. Not to mention the fact that she was too hot, though moments before she'd been sure she was too cold.

She turned on her side and stared at the wall, which at least made a change from staring at the ceiling.

Gage had left a few minutes after six, and she'd barely given him or Clair a thought since. She had better things to do with her time than to wonder how well they were hitting it off.

She had noticed that Gage looked remarkably good when he walked out the door. She'd rarely seen him in anything but jeans, and it had been a mild shock when he'd walked into the kitchen to say goodbye. Wearing a pair of gray slacks and an ice blue shirt open at the throat and with the sleeves rolled halfway up his muscular forearms, he'd looked more like a *GQ* model than the man she knew as her part-time roommate.

When he'd grinned at Danny, she'd seen a more familiar Gage. But then he told the boy that he'd be out past Danny's bedtime so he'd see him in the morning, and it had suddenly occurred to Kelsey that he might be out past *her* bedtime, as well. Maybe he was planning on spending the night with Clair.

The idea had hit her with the force of a blow to the solar plexus, almost literally knocking the breath from her. She'd turned away from him, pretending to fuss with something on the counter while she tried to restore her equilibrium.

The way Clair had maneuvered him into asking her for a date the day before, it wouldn't be surprising if Gage had gotten the impression that dinner and a movie were going to lead straight to Clair's bedroom. For that matter, it was possible that that was exactly what Clair had in mind.

Maybe some signal had passed between the two of them, Kelsey thought as she stared at the shadowy outline of her dresser hours later. She hadn't seen Clair do or say anything to imply that she was willing to entertain an overnight guest but she might have missed it.

She turned over on her back and glared at the ceiling fixture. It was none of her business, she told herself ferociously. Gage and Clair were past the age of consent. They were both smart enough to take the necessary precautions and if they chose to spend the night together, even though they were virtual strangers, it was certainly not her concern.

But the stern mental lecture didn't keep unwanted images from filling her head. Gage kissing Clair with the same passion *she'd* tasted all those months ago. Gage's hands on Clair's body, his leanly muscled frame bent over hers. The two of them sprawled across a bed. Gage touching—

"Stop it!"

The sound of her own voice was shocking in the silent room. Kelsey came up out of bed as if the mattress had suddenly caught fire. She made her way over to the vanity, muttering under her breath when she tripped over a shoe she'd left lying on the carpet. She groped for the switch on the lamp, and a second later soft white light poured out, chasing the shadows into the corners of the room.

She flattened her palms on the polished mahogany of the vanity's surface and stared at her reflection in the oval mirror. What was wrong with her? Gage's sex life—or lack thereof—was none of her business. She'd never even *thought* of him and sex in the same breath—not *ever*.

She avoided her eyes in the mirror, afraid of what she might see in them.

Kelsey began rearranging the scattering of toiletries on top of the vanity, her movements quick and tense. She was just worried about Gage. Gage didn't know Clair, couldn't know what she was like. She could be hard on the men in her life. She expected a great deal from them but wasn't willing to give much herself, which might be at least as much to blame for the failure of her marriage as her ex-husband's fondness for his ancestors.

Kelsey opened the top drawer of the vanity and began rearranging its contents, setting the hairbrush at precise right angles to the box of hairpins, lining her hair clips up in neatly regimented rows.

If she was having a little trouble sleeping, it was just that she was concerned that Gage might get hurt. She picked up a tube of lotion that she'd bought and used once, only to discover that the scent reminded her of overcooked cabbage. And Clair was recently divorced and far from ready to begin a new relationship. The lotion was lined up next to the hairbrush, faceup so that she could see the name clearly. Since she'd introduced the two of them, it was only natural that she'd feel a bit responsible for the outcome of their relationship.

It was a relief to have an explanation for the tangle of emotions that had her awake and rearranging drawers at almost one o'clock in the morning. Being concerned about her friends' happiness was a legitimate excuse for insomnia. It was practically noble of her to be worried about them.

And it was so much safer than thinking that she was jealous of Clair or feeling possessive of Gage. What a ridiculous idea that was!

Kelsey had nearly finished her compulsive reorganization of the drawer when she heard the quiet thud of the front door closing.

He was home! She hadn't heard his car, but since her bedroom was in the back of the house, that wasn't surprising. Her first reaction was relief, so strong that she knew she should be worried by the sheer intensity of it. But for the moment, it was enough to know that he was home, to know he hadn't spent the night with Clair.

Hard on the heels of relief came panic. He had to go past her door to get to the old sun porch that had been converted to a bedroom when he began paying rent. He'd see the light on and think she'd been waiting up for him like a maiden aunt—or a jealous lover.

For a moment, Kelsey stood frozen in place, like a child caught with her hand in the cookie jar. The creak of a floorboard galvanized her into action. She slid the drawer shut abruptly enough to instantly scramble its contents and nearly knocked over the lamp while trying to turn it off. Half convinced that some form of X-ray vision would enable Gage to see through walls and reveal that she wasn't in her bed where any sane woman would be at one o'clock in the morning, Kelsey made a mad dash for the bed. She forgot about the shoes she'd left carelessly lying on the floor until her foot came down on one of them.

She barely managed to muffle her startled shriek when she felt herself start to fall. A second later, she was facedown in the thick, feathery softness of her comforter. But there was no time to give thanks for her gentle landing. She scrambled up the bed, diving under the comforter and pulling it up to her chin.

And then she lay there, staring at the door, holding her breath, her ears so full of the drumming of her own pulse that it was unlikely she'd be able to hear anything less than a dance company wearing tap shoes jogging through the hallway, let alone one man wearing dress shoes. When she heard Gage's bedroom door close a few moments later, the barely audible sound acted like a dash of cold water.

Like a videotape playing on a television screen, Kelsey saw the past few minutes as if from outside herself. Good grief, what was the matter with her? She felt a flush start at her toes and work its way up to her face. Had she lost her mind? If Gage had been a werewolf come to devour her, she couldn't have reacted with more panic.

Her mouth twitched at the image of herself falling over her own shoes, diving under the covers, her heart pounding like that of a schoolgirl caught sneaking home after curfew. A giggle escaped her, loud in the quiet room. She must have looked like a madwoman, she thought, remembering the way she arranged her hair clips with mathematical precision. Kelsey turned, burying her face in her pillow to muffle the sound of her giggles.

"It's not as if I didn't throw myself at him," Clair said. A note of self-mockery came clearly through the phone line.

"You threw yourself at him?" Kelsey's casual tone of voice was belied by her tight grip on the receiver.

"Shamelessly," Clair admitted without embarrassment. "I mean, it's been a long time since I saw quite so much man just walking around loose and unattached. The guy makes the Marlboro Man look like a weeny with a mustache."

"I thought you preferred suave European types." Kelsey twitched the kitchen curtain open to get a better view of the site of the new greenhouse. Gage had borrowed a small backhoe—a toy, he called it—and was leveling the site, preparatory to digging a foundation.

"I had enough of suave and European during my marriage," Clair said, and Kelsey forced her eyes away from Gage. "From now, I'm a strictly 'buy American' kind of girl. If I could lay my hands on a domestic model as gorgeous as Gage Walker, why bother with imports?"

Kelsey laughed, as she knew she was supposed to, but she felt a twinge of irritation at the way Clair made Gage sound like the latest model to roll off a Detroit assembly line. Yes, he was an attractive man but he was also kind and caring and had a great sense of humor. And he deserved someone who appreciated those qualities in him, as well as the more obvious physical attributes.

"It's nice to know you appreciate a man for more than surface qualities," she said dryly.

"The surface is the only thing you can be sure of," Clair said, and there was a wry note in her voice that said she'd learned that lesson the hard way. "Besides, a surface like Gage's is so eminently lookable."

Kelsey couldn't argue with that statement. She just wished that she wasn't suddenly conscious of just how lookable he was. She realized that she was watching him again and turned her back to the window. Annoyed with herself for her preoccupation, she spoke without thinking.

"So why don't you go for it?" she asked Clair. "You're both past the age of consent and free of entanglements. There's nothing stopping you."

Have you lost your mind? a small voice of reason shrieked. Clair was all wrong for Gage. He needed . . . Kelsey's thoughts stumbled as she tried to come up

with just what kind of a woman would be right for
Gage. Nothing came to mind, but she knew he needed
someone other than Clair DiMera, née Miller.

"You haven't been listening, Kelsey," Clair said re-
proachfully. "I threw myself at him, but he wasn't interested in catching."

"He wasn't?" Kelsey realized her tone held an in-
appropriate note of cheer and tried again. "I find that
hard to believe." Which was nothing less than the
truth. For as long as she'd known Clair, she couldn't
ever remember seeing a man resist the other woman's
efforts to charm him.

"Thank you for the kind words. It's too bad Gage
doesn't think I'm as irresistible as you do. Maybe you
should point out the error of his ways," Clair suggested lightly.

"I don't think Gage would appreciate having me
interfere in his love life," Kelsey said.

"Probably not." Clair sighed. "Men tend to think
they actually know what they're doing when it comes
to that sort of thing. Poor, delusional creatures."

Kelsey's laugh was more genuine this time. She really did like Clair. And she refused to think that her
sudden affection for her old friend had anything to do
with the fact that she and Gage were *not* an item.

"I don't know how you've done it," Clair said.

"Done what?" Kelsey asked absently.

Gage had gotten off the backhoe and was bent over,
looking at something on one of the tires. The faded
denim of his jeans molded his lean hips and clung to
the muscled length of his legs in a way that was certainly illegal somewhere.

"I don't know how you've managed to share a house with the man for four years and not jump his bones."

"Not all of us are ruled by our hormones." Kelsey turned her back on the window, thankful that Clair couldn't see the sudden rush of color in her cheeks.

"If you can live with Gage Walker for four years and not knock him over the head and drag him into your bed, you don't *have* any hormones."

"I just don't think of him that way," Kelsey said repressively. At least, she didn't *usually* think of him that way, she added to herself. It was only recently that her thoughts had started drifting in new directions.

"What other way *is* there to think of a man that gorgeous?" Clair asked with such exaggerated amazement that Kelsey laughed.

"Did anyone ever tell you that you've got a one-track mind? If you were a man, you'd be a sexist pig."

"I don't see any reason why a woman can't be a sexist pig," Clair said thoughtfully. "Isn't that what equal rights are all about?"

Kelsey was smiling when she hung up the phone a few minutes later. It really was great to have Clair living nearby again. After she'd married Rick and left Minnesota, they'd corresponded, but letters just weren't the same. She'd almost forgotten how much fun Clair could be.

Her main interest at the moment seemed to be in finding a man to fill the gap left by her divorce. Kelsey shook her head. It was funny, but for all her sophistication and experience, Clair didn't seem to feel complete without a man in her life. The ink was hardly even dry on her divorce decree, and she was already looking for someone new.

As long as that someone wasn't Gage, Kelsey wished her luck.

She realized that she was staring out the window at him again but she didn't move away. He really was a very attractive man. Tall, dark and handsome—the cliché could have been invented to describe Gage Walker.

His thick, dark hair practically invited a woman to run her fingers through it. His shoulders were broad and solid muscle, the kind of shoulders that made a woman feel safe and protected—sheltered. In contrast, his blue eyes offered anything but safety. They held a wicked promise. If the serpent looked at Eve with eyes like that, it was no wonder she took the apple.

She was unaware of her own wistful sigh as she turned away from the window.

Gage saw Kelsey walking toward him with a familiar amber-colored bottle in her hand and reached down to turn off the ignition switch. The engine snorted and snuffled, like a hound complaining about being dragged away from a bowl of kibbles, and then died, leaving behind a welcome silence. He tugged off his baseball cap—a black model adorned with a portrait of Mickey Mouse, a gift from Danny—and hung it over the gearshift before he stepped down off the backhoe.

"You're a lifesaver," he told Kelsey as she reached him. He took the bottle from her and lifted it to his mouth.

"I thought you might be a little thirsty," she said dryly when he lowered the half-empty bottle.

"Just a little." He grinned at her, and she felt a sudden flash of sympathy for Clair. A man with a grin like that really ought to be forced to wear a warning label: Caution—Potential For Heartbreak Ahead.

"So what do you think of the site for your new greenhouse?" He used the bottle to gesture to the bare ground in front of them.

"It looks great. If I'd known how much work it was going to be, I wouldn't have let you talk me into getting it. You're going to spend your whole vacation building my greenhouse. Talk about a busman's holiday."

"I don't mind." Gage surveyed the site with obvious satisfaction. "I usually just see a part of any one job. It's nice to work on something a little smaller."

"So what you're saying is that you're actually enjoying being out here in the hot sun, muscling that machine around in the dust and the heat?"

"Yeah, that's exactly what I'm saying," he admitted with another grin. "Besides, the wages ain't bad." He lifted the bottle for emphasis.

"Top wages, I'm sure," Kelsey said dryly.

"You might be surprised what a man will do for a cold beer on a hot day." He tilted his head back as he brought the bottle to his mouth.

Kelsey watched his throat work as he swallowed, her eyes drifting downward to where a tuft of dark, curly hair rose above the neckline of his faded gray tank top. Sweat had plastered the age-thinned fabric to the muscles of his chest.

He was absolutely, ridiculously male, and Kelsey felt an odd shifting in the pit of her stomach, something that could have been—but wasn't—awareness of him on a male-female level. Clair was right—he did make the Marlboro Man look like a weeny. If he hadn't been such a good friend . . .

"How was your date with Clair?" she blurted out, made uneasy by the direction her own thoughts.

"You asked me that this morning," Gage reminded her as he lowered the bottle. But he was willing to answer it again. "It was fine."

"I forgot," she lied. "I went to bed early, so I don't know what time you got home."

His brows arched a little as if he were puzzled by her interest in his social schedule, but he answered easily enough. "Twelve-thirty or so, I guess."

Kelsey could have corrected him. It had been 12:51, give or take thirty seconds. Not that she'd been counting. She looked past him, focusing her gaze on the backhoe as if fascinated by the scuffed yellow paint.

"I thought you might be out later."

"Dinner and a movie," he said with a shrug. "Not exactly an all-night affair."

The word *affair* made her wince, but she refused to let it deter her. She'd made up her mind that there were things that needed to be said, things that should have been said years ago.

"I thought you might go back to Clair's place—for coffee," she clarified hastily. "That could have run much later."

"Why do I have the sensation that I'm talking to my mother?" Gage asked quizzically.

Kelsey flushed and dragged her eyes back to his face. Obviously it was time to stop beating around the bush and just get the words out. He was looking at her as if he had doubts about her sanity. Who could blame him? She'd had a few doubts herself lately.

"I just wanted you to know that, if you *did* want to stay out later—all night, even—it's none of my business."

"Damn, it really *is* my mother." But there was a darker undercurrent to his light tone that Kelsey chose to ignore.

"We've never talked about it and we should have. I've never given it much thought, but obviously you've got a life to live."

"Gee, thanks."

"You don't answer to me," she persevered, pretending she hadn't heard him. "And I don't want you to think that I expect you to keep...particular hours or anything," she finished lamely.

There was a long silence—an uncomfortable one, which was a rarity between the two of them.

"Does this mean I don't have a curfew anymore?" Gage's tone was less than amused, and Kelsey felt herself flushing.

"I didn't mean it that way."

"No? It sounded suspiciously like you were giving me permission to sleep with your friend Clair."

"Not Clair! I mean, not with Clair, specifically. I just meant...I wanted..." Her voice trailed off as she realized the impossibility of explaining just what it was she'd meant and wanted.

She couldn't bring herself to lift her eyes any higher than the pulse that beat at the base of his throat. Why on earth had she started this conversation? It had seemed so important to let him know that she didn't mind if he had a life apart from her and Danny. Or had she been trying to make that point with herself?

"You know what I meant," she muttered when he didn't seem inclined to break the silence.

"I think I've got a pretty clear picture." Gage downed the last of the beer and set the empty bottle on the backhoe. Hooking his thumbs in the back pockets of his jeans, he stared down at her.

Kelsey glanced up at his face and then away, swallowing a little at the expression in his eyes. He looked very large, very male and very irritated. This had not been one of her better ideas. Gage obviously agreed.

"What you're trying to tell me is that if I want to have wild, mindless sex with a woman I don't know, I don't have to call to let you know I'm going to be late."

Kelsey's flush deepened painfully. It would have been impossible to say which bothered her more: the heavy sarcasm in his tone or the image of Gage's having wild, mindless sex with another woman.

"That's not what I meant," she mumbled, knowing it was more or less what she'd meant.

"Does the lecture on safe sex come next?" he asked in a ferociously light tone. "Aren't you going to caution me about the hazards of dating in the nineties?"

Gage wasn't sure why he was so angry. There was something about having Kelsey tell him that she didn't mind if he wanted to spend the night with another woman that touched a nerve.

"I didn't mean to make it sound as if I was giving you permission to spend the night with someone," she protested. "I was just trying to tell you that I wouldn't...that it's not... Oh, hell. I'm not doing this very well." She stared down at her feet, poking the toe of her sandal in the raw dirt.

"It depends on what you're trying to do."

Gage's anger was tempered by her obvious discomfort. Or maybe it was that he'd been suddenly struck by how vulnerable she looked. Her hair was drawn up in a ponytail, leaving baby-fine curls of pale gold lying against her nape. He had a sudden memory of what it had felt like to slide his fingers through those curls, to curve his palm around the back of her neck. A year and a half later, the memories were sharp and vivid. He looked away from her, his anger muffled by discomfort at the direction his thoughts were taking.

Kelsey sighed, breaking the uneasy little silence. Tilting her head back, she gave him a rueful smile.

"All I'm trying to say is that I know you have a life apart from Danny and me. I guess these past few years I've sometimes forgotten that. You've been so good to us, giving me money—"

"I'm paying rent."

"—and doing work on the house."

"I live here, too."

"Looking after Danny."

"Not exactly a hardship."

"And now spending your vacation putting up a greenhouse for me."

"Saint Gage, that's what everyone calls me," he muttered. He shifted uncomfortably, wishing she'd stop making it sound as if he were sacrificing his life. He *wanted* to spend time with Danny. And he liked working on the house. It was a nice change to see a project through from start to finish, even if it was something as simple as replacing a closet door.

"I just don't want you to think that *I* think that Danny and I have some kind of exclusive right to your time when you're home. And I don't want you to feel like you have to check in with me when you're out, if you wanted to…stay out all night or anything. I mean, I'm not your den mother, right?"

Gage didn't return her forced smile. He was trying to figure out just what it was about this conversation that was so irritating. He knew what she was trying to say. She was actually trying to make him more comfortable. A better man would have appreciated her efforts, he supposed. But there was something about having Kelsey give him permission to date other women—to sleep with them even—that touched a nerve he hadn't known he had.

He spoke slowly. "So, you're telling me that, if I go out for the evening and don't come home all night, you're not going to worry?"

Kelsey opened her mouth to say yes and closed it without speaking. Gage saw the sudden flash of pain in her eyes and knew she was remembering the night Rick had died. He immediately regretted the question. He hadn't meant to remind her of that.

"I'd worry," she admitted slowly. "But that's not your problem. You shouldn't have to check in with me. I'm your roommate, not your mother. No matter how I may have sounded a few minutes ago."

"So I should just ignore the fact that you may be wondering if it's time to call the hospitals and continue having a good time?" He didn't add anything more. He didn't have to. He watched as his words sank in.

"Maybe I didn't think things through as well as I should have," she admitted after a moment. "Believe it or not, my intentions were good."

"I believe it. And I appreciate your sudden concern for my love life, but it's really not necessary."

"You should just tell me to mind my own business."

"Mind your own business." But his teasing smile took any possible sting from the words.

"Could we just forget this whole conversation ever happened?"

"What conversation?"

Kelsey laughed and the awkward moment was over, if not actually forgotten.

A few minutes later, Gage watched her walk back to the house. What had brought on her sudden attention to his social life? His eyes lingered on the gentle swing of her hips beneath snug pink cotton shorts. For such a small woman, she certainly had plenty of curves. And they were in all the right places.

With an effort, he dragged his gaze from her and turned away. Settling into the backhoe's seat, he reminded himself that Kelsey wasn't just an attractive woman. She was his best friend's wife.

But the reminder wasn't quite enough to banish the memory of how soft her mouth had tasted and how right she'd felt in his arms.

Chapter 7

The week after their discussion was a particularly busy one for Kelsey, which was probably just as well, since it gave her less time to dwell on her sudden, inexplicable fascination with Gage's social life. Mid-June was a peak harvest season, not to mention weed season. The gardens soaked up as much time as Kelsey could give them. She was grateful that it was work that she truly loved but she wouldn't have minded spending a few less hours at it.

As if the gardens didn't keep her busy enough, there was Danny's trip to prepare for. Every summer for the past four years, the two of them had made the trip to Minnesota to see her parents. This year, with the new greenhouse going up and the gardens bursting with produce, Kelsey hadn't felt as if she could afford two weeks away from home. But she hadn't wanted to deprive her parents or her son of the chance to spend time together so she'd decided to send Danny alone.

It had seemed like a good idea at the time. Danny was six now and sensible for his age. And it wasn't as if he'd *really* be traveling alone. She'd hand him over to an attendant, who'd keep an eye on him during the flight, and her parents would meet the plane in Minneapolis. There was nothing to worry about.

But now that the time had arrived, Kelsey was suddenly stricken with doubts. If it hadn't been for Danny's excitement at the prospect of doing something so enormously grown-up, not to mention the shameless spoiling he knew awaited him in Minnesota, she would have called off the whole thing. Instead, she wept into the suitcase she packed for him and hugged him so often that he started to give her a wary look whenever she got close to him.

It was a good thing Gage drove them to the airport, because Kelsey was too busy trying to hold back tears to watch the road. Danny, with a heartlessness possible only in a child of six, chatted happily all the way to Los Angeles, delighted at the prospect of visiting his grandparents and showing no sign of apprehension at the thought of traveling alone. Once at the airport and waiting for his flight, he was less interested in savoring the last few minutes with his mother than he was in watching the planes take off and land.

When his flight was called, he shot out of his seat as if propelled by rockets.

"It's time!" He would have dashed onto the plane unassisted if Gage hadn't made a quick grab for his shoulder. Kelsey shot him a grateful look as she took Danny's hand and walked him over to the flight attendant.

"You're squeezing my hand," Danny complained loudly.

Squeezing his hand? It was all she could do to keep from snatching him into her arms and rushing from the airport with him. Why had she agreed to this? Why hadn't she told her parents that they'd just have to wait until later in the year when she'd be able to accompany him? What kind of a wretched parent was she?

"He's going to be fine," Gage said from beside her as the flight attendant led Danny into the jetway.

"He's so little," Kelsey whispered. "What if he gets scared and I'm not there?"

As if on cue, Danny turned and waved cheerfully just before walking out of sight. Kelsey promptly burst into tears.

Gage put his arm around her shoulders and led her to an out-of-the-way corner.

"He's going to be just fine," he told her again.

"I shouldn't have let him go," she muttered into his shirtfront.

"The airlines take good care of kids traveling alone. They'll spoil him all the way to Minnesota." He patted her back soothingly.

"I should have gone with him."

"You've got a business to run."

"It shouldn't come ahead of Danny."

"Time and beets wait for no woman," he intoned solemnly, but Kelsey was momentarily beyond appreciating his humor. Wallowing in maternal guilt, she was not so easily distracted.

"I'm a terrible mother," she said tragically.

The extravagance of that claim gave him pause. "Because you're sending Danny to be hopelessly spoiled by his grandparents?" he asked, arching one brow in question.

Kelsey shook her head as she drew away from him. Opening her purse, she began to dig through it, looking for a tissue. "Because I was actually...looking forward to him being gone for a...a little while." Her breath hitched on a sob. "I thought I'd enjoy some time a...lone." She sniffed and rifled her purse more urgently. "What kind of a mother looks forward to getting rid of her six-year-old son?"

"One who values her sanity," he said dryly. When she didn't smile, he sighed and took a more serious approach. "It's not like you're sending him to work on a chain gang. Your parents aren't going to tie him to the bed and feed him bread and water, are they?"

"N-no." She sniffed harder and dug deeper into her purse. If she couldn't find a tissue, she'd settle for a crumpled napkin. "They'll spoil him rotten."

"Then what's your problem?" Gage tugged her fingers out of the way and reached into her purse to pull out an only slightly crumpled napkin bearing the insignia of a fast-food restaurant. "Blow your nose and wake up and smell the coffee. You've got two weeks of freedom. Two weeks without having every meal critiqued by someone who thinks Oscar Mayer is the world's greatest chef and a bologna sandwich is the height of culinary achievement."

That drew a choked laugh from her. "He's not a very adventurous eater, is he?"

"An understatement, to put it mildly. I've seen rocks with better taste." Gage waited while she dried her eyes and blew her nose. "Feeling better?"

"Yes." She managed a smile that wavered only slightly around the edges. "I suppose you think I'm an idiot."

"Yeah. Lucky for you, I like idiots." He slung his arm around her shoulders and turned her toward the windows. "Once he's in the air, let's blow this joint. On the way home, let's have dinner someplace where they put real silverware on the table."

"No plastic?" she asked wistfully. She couldn't remember the last time she'd eaten in a place where the food didn't come in paper bags.

"No plastic," he vowed.

It could have been the promise of eating real, grown-up food that enabled Kelsey to watch Danny's plane taxi away from the terminal without shedding more tears, but she thought it more likely that it was the warmth of Gage's arm around her shoulders. She leaned her head against his shoulder and thought again that she was lucky to have him.

It was the first time that Kelsey could remember the big kitchen actually feeling crowded. But there probably weren't many rooms that could hold Gage *and* his brothers without getting just a little cramped. They were so... large. And loud.

Keefe, Cole, Sam and Sam's wife, Nikki, had arrived before the sun, prepared to spend the day putting up her greenhouse. An old-fashioned barn raising, Gage had said when he told her what he had planned. Kelsey had been touched that his family would be willing to give up their weekend for her. But she was starting to think they had less interest in putting up a greenhouse than they did in the round of good-natured arguing that had been going on since their arrival.

Cradling mugs of coffee, they stood around her kitchen, arguing about what was the best way to start the day's job. If she'd thought there was only one way to raise a greenhouse, she was rapidly disabused of that fantasy. Apparently there were at least four ways.

"I say we assemble the sides on the ground and then set them in place," Cole was saying. Fair haired and dark eyed, he resembled Gage only in height and general bone structure.

"That's why you're a pilot and not a builder," Keefe said bluntly. "That'll never work."

"And I suppose you know a better way?" Cole asked with heavy sarcasm. "Last I heard, you're a rancher, not a contractor. This isn't a cow we're branding."

"We put up a barn on my place last year, and it hasn't fallen down yet." Keefe lifted his mug and took a swallow of coffee. Kelsey found Keefe Walker a little intimidating. Tall like his brothers, with nearly black hair and eyes the color of bittersweet chocolate, there was an air of reserve about him, as if he kept a certain distance between himself and the world.

"One barn doesn't exactly make you Frank Lloyd Wright," Sam said with a grin.

Keefe raised his brows and gave his older brother an inquiring look. "I suppose being a cop has given you extensive experience in putting up greenhouses?"

"Not exactly. But it's given me problem-solving skills that the rest of you don't have."

His brothers promptly booed him into silence. He shrugged, not in the least disturbed by their lack of appreciation. "You always did resent me because I was the eldest."

"We resented you because you were the most obnoxious," Gage told him.

"Pure jealousy," Sam said sadly. He shot a martyred look across the room at his wife. "You see what I've put up with?"

"You're a sad specimen," Nikki agreed without noticeable sympathy. "A bit overwhelming, aren't they?" she said to Kelsey as the four men began to squabble again.

"A bit," Kelsey admitted, smiling at her. This was the first time she'd met Nikki Walker but she already liked the other woman.

"One of them is almost too much. When you get all four of them together, it's downright frightening. All that testosterone in a confined space—" She shuddered. "If the surgeon general ever finds out about it, he'll probably forbid them to gather in groups of more than two." Nikki's green eyes sparkled with humor.

Kelsey chuckled. "Maybe he'd just slap a warning label on them."

"Prolonged Exposure Can Cause Heart Palpitations And Dizziness," Nikki suggested. "I can testify to that," she said softly, giving her husband a look that made it clear she didn't object to the symptoms.

Kelsey's eyes drifted to where Gage stood, one hip braced against the counter as he listened to his brothers argue. Dizziness and palpitations? She could certainly imagine Gage's causing symptoms like that. Those electric blue eyes of his were alone enough to make a woman's pulse beat a little faster. Not to mention a body that would have made Michelangelo itch for a chisel and a hunk of marble.

She realized that Nikki was watching her and shifted her gaze from Gage's tall figure. Kelsey met the speculative look in the other woman's eyes and flushed a little. On the pretext of reaching for the coffeepot, she turned away. The fact that she noticed Gage's attractiveness didn't mean what Nikki's expression said it meant, she thought, feeling a little defensive.

Despite popular opinion, it *was* possible for a man and a woman to be friends. Even when the man in question was devastatingly good-looking and had a smile that was pure charm.

"You're *all* wrong." Gage's announcement pulled Kelsey's attention back to him.

"According to whom?" Cole asked, arching one brow.

"Me. I've already got everything figured out. We can get started as soon as you guys are done arguing." He drained his coffee cup before setting it on the counter.

"Why should we do it your way?" Sam asked.

"Because I've built a lot more bridges than you guys have," Gage said.

"That would be pretty impressive if we were putting up a bridge," Keefe drawled. "But a greenhouse isn't exactly first cousin to a bridge."

"True." Gage nodded as if that hadn't occurred to him until now. "But I have something none of you have. Besides wit and charm, of course."

The chorus of disgusted groans that followed had both Kelsey and Nikki grinning.

"What you've got is a swelled head," Cole muttered.

"Maybe. But I also have something more useful." Gage waited a moment, his mouth curving in a grin that held pure devilment. He picked up the manila folder lying next to him on the counter and waved it tauntingly. "I've got the instructions from the manufacturer."

* * *

It had to be a hundred degrees in the shade, Gage thought. He said as much to Cole, who was sprawled in the redwood chaise longue next to his.

"Ninety," Cole corrected him, squinting at the big round thermometer Kelsey had hanging on the back porch.

Gage shook his head. "Gotta be hotter than that. I'm too wiped out for it to be under a hundred."

"Maybe you shouldn't have eaten that second serving of strawberry shortcake," Keefe suggested without bothering to open his eyes. "A man eats too much, it's likely to make him sluggish."

"I didn't notice you exercising much restraint," Gage retorted. "How many sandwiches did you put away, anyway?"

The three of them were resting in the shade of a huge live oak. Sam and Nikki were walking through Kelsey's gardens, but since they were holding hands and their heads were bent close together, no one was fooled into thinking they were admiring the produce.

It was Sunday afternoon, and the greenhouse was nearly complete. A day and a half of work had left everyone pleasantly exhausted and well satisfied with the results of their labor.

"Does she always cook like that?" Cole asked.

"She likes to cook," Gage said by way of an answer.

"It's a good thing you're gone most of the year. If you ate like this all the time, you'd weigh three hundred pounds," Cole said. "I feel like a turkey, stuffed and ready to go in the oven."

"Nobody told you to take that last sandwich," Keefe countered.

"I didn't see you turning anything down."

"I'm not dumb." Keefe shook his head. "I'm not much of a cook, and Jace can burn boiling water. We survive on TV dinners. I'm going to enjoy this while I can. It may be the last decent food I eat between now and Thanksgiving."

"Maybe you should take a doggie bag home for Jace," Gage suggested. Jace Reno was Keefe's partner on the Flying Ace Ranch.

"Better not. One taste of Kelsey's cooking and he'll probably hotfoot it down here and offer to marry her," Keefe said.

"*Somebody* ought to marry her," Cole said. "Any woman who can cook like that is a woman worth marrying."

"You're a little behind the times, aren't you?" Gage asked, feeling an odd twinge of annoyance. They might be joking, but this was Kelsey they were talking about. "Men don't marry women for their cooking these days."

Cole and Keefe exchanged glances and then looked at their brother. "Why not?"

The perfect blankness of the question drew a snort of laughter. "I guess it's too late to try and drag you guys into the twentieth century."

"Don't kid yourself," Keefe said. "Men want the same thing from a woman in the twentieth century that they always have. Food—"

"And sex," Cole finished for him.

"What about intellectual stimulation?"

"If I want my intellect stimulated, I'll watch 'Jeopardy,'" Cole said.

"Companionship?"

"I get that from my horse," Keefe said.

"Children?"

"I've got Mary," Cole said, referring to his six-year-old daughter. "One's enough."

"I'll borrow one if the urge for fatherhood ever strikes," Keefe offered.

"So a woman's only good for food and sex?" Gage asked them.

"Well…" Cole narrowed his eyes and pretended to think about it. He glanced at Keefe as if in consultation. "It would be kind of nice to have someone to clean the house."

There was a long pause, and then the three of them burst out laughing.

"If Mom heard the two of you talking that way…" Gage said, chuckling.

"Don't tell her!" Cole widened his eyes in a look of exaggerated fear. "She'd wash our mouths out with soap."

"Worse, she'd give us that look," Keefe said.

All three brothers were momentarily silent as they contemplated the power of Rachel Walker's "look." The combination of love and disappointment in that particular look had been enough to bring the most rebellious teenager into line and have him willing to do almost anything to erase it from her eyes. She'd never had to raise her hand to them. The look had been much more effective.

Cole shuddered. "Anything but that."

"Anything but what?" Sam asked, arriving in time to hear his brother's comment.

"Gage was threatening to tell Mom that she raised a bunch of male chauvinist pigs," Keefe said. He moved his legs to the side of the chaise longue, making a place for his older brother to sit down.

"You always were a stool pigeon." Sam frowned at Gage.

"Me? Who was it who told Dad that Cole and I were on the garage roof?"

"I was trying to save your miserable little hides," Sam protested.

"After Dad got through with us, I don't think there was a whole hell of a lot of hide left," Cole said, smiling reminiscently.

"So what brought on the accusations of chauvinist piggery?" Sam asked.

"Cole and I pointed out that the primary advantages of marriage are having someone else to do the cooking and not having to sleep alone," Keefe said.

"And someone to clean," Cole added solemnly.

"I suggested that some men might look for other things in a marriage," Gage said.

"What else is there?" Sam asked in a tone of blank surprise.

Gage groaned while Cole and Keefe hooted with laughter.

"If you ever tell Nikki I said that, I'll have you all arrested," Sam threatened, grinning.

"You've got her fooled into thinking you're an enlightened male?" Cole asked.

"Yeah." Sam's eyes sought out Nikki where she stood talking with Kelsey on the back porch. "I'd hate for her to find out the truth before our first anniversary."

The look in his eyes made it obvious that he adored his wife. Keefe nudged him with the toe of his boot. "You'd keep her even if she couldn't cook," he accused gently.

"She can't," he admitted with a grin. "Lucky for both of us, Lena does all the cooking." Lena had fulfilled the roles of cook, housekeeper and part-time mother since Nikki was a child. They fell into a comfortable silence. The four of them had always been close. Their father, David Walker, had been a police officer. He'd been killed in the line of duty when his oldest son, Sam, was twelve years old and Cole, the youngest, was only seven. The tragedy had served to create bonds between the four boys that had lasted into adulthood.

It was Cole who broke the silence. "You know, it doesn't seem fair. Not only does she cook like a dream but she's got legs that make a man's mouth water."

"Who?" Gage asked, as if he hadn't been staring at Kelsey's legs himself.

"Kelsey." Cole slanted him a look that questioned his sanity. "Don't tell me you've never noticed her legs."

Gage answered with a shrug. It seemed the safest response.

"You had your eyes checked lately?" Keefe asked without opening his eyes.

"Kelsey's a friend of mine," Gage said repressively.

"What's that got to do with it?" Cole asked, giving him another of those questioning looks. "She's a friend of mine, too, and *I* noticed she had great legs."

"She's Rick's wife." Even as Gage said it, he realized how ridiculous it sounded. Cole's arched eyebrow made it clear he agreed.

"Rick's been dead for four years," Keefe stated quietly.

"Yeah, well..." There wasn't much Gage could say to that, so he shrugged and sat up. He knew Rick was dead, knew Kelsey was his widow, not his wife. It was just that Gage still thought of her as being married to Rick, as being out of reach. Didn't he?

Suddenly uncomfortable, he picked up his glass from the ground next to the chaise and looked at it as if surprised to find it empty. "I'm going to get some more lemonade and then get back to work."

His brothers watched him walk away. Cole glanced at Sam and Keefe. There was a gleam of laughter in his eyes. "You think he hadn't noticed Kelsey's legs?"

"He noticed," Sam said, his eyes still on Gage.

"I don't think there's much about her he hasn't noticed," Keefe added as Gage pulled open the screen door and stepped into the house and out of sight.

Gage *had* noticed Kelsey's legs. Long and slim and tanned—it was damned hard *not* to notice them. Especially when she was wearing a pair of skimpy little cutoffs that left so much of them bare. He pulled open the refrigerator and stared inside but he wasn't seeing the jumbled array of food. What he saw was the way the faded cutoffs molded themselves to Kelsey's bottom, the smooth length of leg beneath—ridiculously long legs for such a small woman.

The word he muttered was short, pungent and almost drowned out by the sound of the refrigerator door slamming shut. Damn Cole for mentioning Kelsey's legs, Gage thought, ignoring the fact that he'd noticed them long before his brother mentioned them. The thought made him scowl. What the hell had Cole been doing looking at her legs, anyway?

The sound of laughter brought him to the back door. Kelsey and Nikki were standing under the big

oak, talking to his brothers. Nikki was perched on
Sam's knee, his arms looped around her waist, the
picture of wedded bliss. But Gage's attention was
caught by the fact that Cole was no longer lying back
on the redwood chaise but was now standing talking
to Kelsey. Even as he watched, Cole said something
that made Kelsey laugh, the sound of it carrying easily across the few yards to the house.

Gage's teeth clenched, and he reached for the door,
intending to go out and put a stop to... Put a stop to
what? The question made him pause. Put a stop to his
younger brother's charming Kelsey? Cole and Kelsey? A couple? His jaw tightened, but he forced himself to roll the thought over in his mind.

Reluctantly he admitted that there was no reason the
two of them shouldn't be more than friends. As far as
he knew, Cole hadn't been involved in a serious relationship since his divorce five years before. As a single father, he was careful about dating, not wanting to
let Mary get fond of a woman only to have her walk
out of their lives the way Mary's mother had. Kelsey
would make a terrific mother for Mary, just as Cole
would be a great father for Danny. Any sane person
would be glad to think they'd found each other.

So what does that make you, Walker?

There was another burst of laughter from the group
under the tree, and it struck Gage that he was over-
reacting, to put it mildly. A few laughs with some
friends, and he practically had Kelsey and Cole married and living happily ever after. He shook his head
as he pushed open the screen door and stepped out
onto the porch. Obviously he'd spent too many hours
in the sun today.

Chapter 8

Kelsey spread her arms as if she could embrace the structure that stood in the moonlight. She had her greenhouse. Two solid days of work, and the Walker men had built a piece of her dreams. It gleamed under the light of a full moon, built like the upturned keel of a Viking ship, arched and curved, coming to a peak at the top. It was a thing of beauty and it was hers.

There were still some details to be finished—benches to be built, heating and cooling to fine-tune, watering systems to install, and it would take months of experimentation to learn what she could and couldn't grow but that was the fun part. The heart of the dream was sitting in front of her, solid and real.

"What are you doing?"

Kelsey started at the sound of Gage's voice. She spun around, one hand pressed to her chest as if to still her pounding heart. He was standing in the kitchen, looking at her through the screen door. Recovered from her surprise, she gave him a smile that held a touch of embarrassment.

"I'm looking at the greenhouse."

"At three o'clock in the morning?" He stifled a yawn.

"I was too excited to sleep," she admitted sheepishly.

"It's not exactly ready for you to start planting," he pointed out dryly. The screen door creaked as he pushed it open and joined her on the porch.

"I know. But it will be." Kelsey turned back to the greenhouse. In her mind's eye, it was already full of greenery—seedlings for the garden and extras to sell. Maybe she'd even try growing some houseplants to market.

"If that isn't just like an executive, always looking for new ways to make money," Gage said, making her realize that she'd been detailing her plans out loud.

She laughed. "I guess I am CEO of this operation. Not to mention treasurer, head gardener, secretary and janitor."

"Before too long, I expect to see your empire spreading up and down the state. Today a greenhouse. Tomorrow the world." He swept his hands out in an expansive gesture.

Kelsey laughed again, but it sounded strained to her ears. She was uncomfortably aware that it took a conscious effort to turn her eyes away from his bare chest and the corded muscles of his shoulders. She focused determinedly on her new greenhouse. She'd seen Gage shirtless before. There was nothing unusual in that. If her pulse was beating a little faster, it was excitement over the greenhouse.

"I'll settle for a little piece of the Santa Ynez Valley, thank you. I don't want the whole state."

"It's probably about to fall into the Pacific anyway," Gage said, nodding his agreement.

She smiled but the look she gave him was serious. "I can't thank you enough, Gage. You, Sam, Keefe and Cole, all of you spending your whole weekend putting this up for me." She gestured to indicate the graceful building. "I still can't believe it's here. And I can't believe you guys did all this for me."

"We had fun," Gage told her.

It was nothing more than the truth, he thought, glancing at the greenhouse. It had been hard work, but he'd enjoyed himself and he knew his brothers had, too. And even if he'd hated every minute of it, it would have been worth it for the look in Kelsey's eyes right now. She looked like a child seeing the fulfillment of a Christmas wish, her eyes shining, her expression bright with happiness.

It struck him suddenly that he'd never seen her look prettier. Her hair was a pale silvery gold in the moonlight as it fell in tousled waves to her shoulders. He knew what it would feel like curling over his fingers, strands of fine silk thread. Gage pushed his hands in his pockets, taking them out of temptation's way.

Kelsey was wearing a soft cotton robe in a color that hovered between blue and green. It was ankle length, belted at the waist and modest as a nun's habit, obviously designed for comfort rather than seduction. He'd seen her wear it before, but tonight he found himself noticing the pale wedge of skin visible at the base of her throat and the way the belt tied at the waist emphasized the womanly curves of her.

"I'm glad you like the greenhouse," he said, needing to break the silence.

"Like it?" Kelsey shook her head, laughing at his understatement. "I love it!"

"Good." The floral scent of her shampoo drifted to him, mingling with the warm, earthy smell of the gardens and the sharp tang of wood and sealant from the new greenhouse. His fingers curled into his palms, clenched fists pushing against the fabric of his jeans.

This was Kelsey, he reminded himself. He wasn't supposed to notice things like her scent and the way the fabric of her robe clung to her body. He wasn't supposed to remember how soft her skin was or the taste of her mouth. And he wasn't supposed to think about what it would be like to kiss her again. Or how she might look stretched out on his bed, her hair tumbled over his pillow, her gray eyes smoky with desire.

"Oh, Gage, thank you so much!" Unable to contain her excitement a moment longer, Kelsey turned and put her hands on his shoulders, standing up on tiptoes to press a kiss on his cheek.

Gage reacted automatically, pulling his hands out of his pockets and settling them on the gentle swell of her hips to steady her. It was not perhaps the best time for him to find himself with his arms full of warm, sweet-smelling woman. Not when that woman was Kelsey and when his thoughts had just been drifting down forbidden paths. And particularly not when it felt so very right to be holding her.

Too right, he thought as his fingers tightened, drawing her subtly closer. Her mouth brushed his cheek. Without thinking, he turned his head, and their lips were suddenly less than a whisper apart.

Their eyes met, gray crossing blue. Time stopped. They stared at each other, years of friendship peeling away to expose a deep-rooted hunger that had lain there, unrecognized, unacknowledged. Kelsey's breathing took on a ragged edge. She shifted slightly, her body brushing against Gage's, her fingers curling into the muscles of his shoulders.

Awareness slammed into them, sending thoughts of friendship and right and wrong spinning away. Gage felt hunger grab him by the throat, a need so powerful it rocked him all the way to his soul. In Kelsey's eyes was the same need, the same awareness. Her body curved to his, softening in some indefinable way, bending to him as a willow might bend before a wind too powerful to resist.

He made no conscious decision to kiss her, but suddenly her mouth was yielding to his, her lips opening for him like a flower opening to welcome the life-giving rain.

She drank in the taste of him, the strength of him. So long, she thought. She'd needed this for so long, wanted him forever. Her fingers burrowed into the thick darkness of his hair, pulling him closer, and she realized even as she did so that he could never be close enough.

She had no idea how long they stood there in the moonlight, wrapped in hunger and soft night air. Gage's mouth devoured hers, as if he were a starving man suddenly presented with a feast. And her own hunger was every bit as great. She couldn't get enough of the taste of him, the smell of him, the feel of him.

"Kelsey." Her name was a groan, a whisper of sound as Gage dragged his mouth from hers.

She felt a whimper of protest catch in her throat as she forced her eyes open and stared up at him. "Gage?"

The blatant hunger in her eyes was his undoing. He'd thought vaguely to end this before it was too late, before things went too far. But one look at her face, her lips softly swollen from his kisses, her eyes languorous and smoky with arousal, and he knew it hadn't gone nearly far enough.

He couldn't stop it, he thought, and a feeling of both exultation and despair swept over him. He had to have her. Come hell or high water, this had to happen. There'd be a price to pay later. He knew that but it didn't matter. He'd worry about it afterward. Later he'd walk through hell if he had to but he couldn't turn his back on this taste of heaven.

Kelsey saw the flicker of emotions chase one another across his face and she wondered what he was thinking, wondered if he was going to turn away from the magic of this moment, going to leave them both aching and empty and force her to spend yet another night alone. She held her breath, waiting.

"Hold on," he said as he bent to slide one arm behind her knees.

Kelsey wound her arms around his neck and lowered her head to his chest, listening to the strong beat of his heart as he carried her inside.

Gage found his way through the darkened house and into his bedroom by blind instinct. All his senses were wrapped up in the woman in his arms. He carried her to the bed, lowering her to stand beside it, his hands reaching for the belt of her robe.

He told himself he should slow down. He wanted this to last forever, wanted to savor every moment, taste every inch of soft skin revealed by the robe as it slid down her body. But the pulse drumming in his ears made it impossible to think, impossible to slow his hands as they swept the robe from her shoulders, letting it drop to the floor to pool around her feet.

Despite the urgency he felt, Gage's hands stilled as he looked at her. There was a small lamp burning on the nightstand, casting a shallow wash of light over the two of them, illuminating the curves of Kelsey's body. She was perfection. She was the fulfillment of fantasies he'd never allowed himself to admit to having. She was woman personified.

And for this moment at least, she was his.

The very strength of his desire startled Gage into a momentary awareness of what was happening, of how this would change things. But then Kelsey reached for the snap at the top of his jeans, and he knew it was too late to stop what was happening. Need roared through him, hard and powerful, driving out the last tattered remnants of sanity, leaving only the hunger that pounded in his veins. Maybe it had been too late from the moment they touched. Or even before that, when he'd followed her outside.

It didn't matter. Nothing mattered but finding a way to feed this hunger, to soothe the ache that made his hands shake as he lowered her to the bed, following her down onto the tangled covers. He had to have her, no matter what the cost later.

Kelsey gasped at the feel of Gage's lean body against hers. He was so hot. His skin burned as if with fever. She felt an echo of that heat deep inside—a heavy, liquid warmth that settled low and deep, making her achingly aware of an emptiness that only he could fill. She was aware of his jerking open the nightstand drawer and then the crackle of plastic as he opened the condom. She thought vaguely that she should be grateful that he retained enough sanity to think of birth control but all she felt was impatience. She needed him. *Now.* She moved restlessly beneath him, her legs opening to cradle him as he lowered himself over her.

"Too fast," he whispered hoarsely, struggling to slow the moment even as his hardness brushed against the damp heat of her.

"Now," she begged. Her hands found his hips, her fingers digging into his skin as she arched her body in silent demand. "Now. Please, Gage. Now."

And with a groan, he gave her what she wanted, what they both had to have. With one powerful thrust, he sheathed himself in her waiting warmth. She cried out, her body arching in shocked pleasure, the movement taking him deeper still until they were so closely joined that it was as if they were two halves of the same whole.

Gage pressed his forehead to her shoulder, struggling for control. He should stop, should slow this down, should... Kelsey arched beneath him, her fingers digging into his hips in a silent plea, and he stopped trying to control what was happening between them. He had a better chance of roping a hurricane or stopping the world from turning.

Bracing himself on his elbows, he began to move within her. It was hard and fast, an explosive coming-together that reached soul deep, wrenching forth a powerful response like nothing he'd ever known.

The delicate ripple of feminine muscles caressing him, welcoming his invasion, was a pleasure so intense that it hovered on the knife edge of pain. He wanted it to last forever. But Kelsey was already arching beneath him, her slender body taut as a bowstring, her nails digging into his hips as she tumbled headlong into fulfillment. With a groan, Gage followed her into the spinning tumult, pouring himself into her, shuddering with the intensity of the moment.

The silence that followed seemed as abrupt and unexpected as the passion that had preceded it. Kelsey felt a delicious languor creep over her, replacing the urgency. Drained of strength and willpower, she kept her mind a deliberate blank, savoring the feel of Gage's big body over her, within her. She slid one hand up his back, her fingers drifting along the ridge of his spine. She felt as if she could lie here forever, hardly breathing, just savoring the feeling of completion that spread through her body.

She shifted slightly and heard Gage's breath catch. Experimentally she moved again, tightening her inner muscles around him, feeling him stir and start to swell within her. A moment before, she'd have sworn that the slow tumble of renewed hunger wasn't possible, that not even movement was possible. But her body was softening, her skin tingling with awareness.

"Kelsey." Her name was a protest. A plea.

"Gage." His name was an affirmation. A plea.

And it began to build again.

It didn't seem possible, but the hunger—the need—was just as great the second time. They feasted on each other, hands and mouths, touching, kissing, exploring, almost fighting each other in their urgency.

Gage moved over her, his hands cupping her buttocks, tilting her so that she took him deeper still. Kelsey cried out, her body shuddering as her climax took her, tumbling her headlong into a shimmering pool of sensation. But Gage continued to thrust, driving her higher and higher, the pleasure building to an almost frightening intensity.

Her teeth sank into his shoulder, her breath coming in deep, panting sobs as she struggled to retain at least a fingertip hold on reality. But Gage wouldn't allow even that. His hand slid between them, finding the tiny bud at the top of her womanhood and stroking it with his thumb.

And Kelsey came apart in his arms. She would have screamed if she'd had the breath to do so. But he'd stolen her breath, stolen her ability to think. She arched, taking him deeper, so deep that she could feel him in her very soul. He shuddered and she felt the throb and pulse of his climax deep inside her.

And then they were spinning down from the mountaintop, just the two of them alone in all the universe.

It was a long, long time before either of them moved, and an eternity before Gage gathered the strength to lift himself away from her. Kelsey murmured a protest when he left the bed and went into the bathroom. But he was back before she could form a coherent complaint. He slid back into bed, easing his arm under her neck and pulling her against his side. Her head settled into the hollow of his shoulder, her body curving around his as if they'd lain together like this a thousand times.

Gage threaded his fingers through her hair, feeling it curl around his fingers like strands of pale gold silk. He couldn't remember the last time he'd felt so completely relaxed, so totally fulfilled.

That it should be Kelsey who'd made him feel that way was stunning. He shifted, some of his contentment fading.

"Kelsey?"

She didn't respond immediately, and for a moment, he thought that she might pretend to be asleep. Then she stirred slightly, tucking her head more solidly against his chest.

"What?"

There was a wariness in her tone that made him hesitate. What had just happened meant . . .

Hell, he didn't know what it meant and he realized suddenly that he didn't want to know, didn't want to think about it. There were things that needed to be said, things they had to talk about, but not now. Right now all he wanted was to hold Kelsey, to savor the feel of her lying next to him.

"Nothing. Just Kelsey."

"Good," she whispered, and he knew she didn't want to let reality intrude on this moment any more than he did. He eased his fingers through her hair again, letting the contentment seep back over him. He was suddenly, overwhelmingly tired. They'd talk in the morning, he promised himself as he drifted off to sleep.

Chapter 9

Kelsey came awake slowly, reluctantly. There was a distant, pounding noise that faded away even as she woke so that it seemed part of a dream she'd been having, forgotten even before she was completely awake.

The covers were too heavy, she thought fretfully. They were pressing her against the mattress. She moved to push them away from her but found herself grabbing hold of a solid, male arm that lay across her waist, pinning her to the bed. Still half-asleep, she trailed her fingers upward, her fingertips tracing hard muscle and hair-dusted skin until she reached his shoulder. He was lying on his stomach, she decided dreamily, one arm thrown across her.

She shifted uneasily. Rick never sprawled onto her side of the bed. He never cuddled up with her to go to sleep, preferring to have plenty of space. That was why they'd bought such a big bed, even though it crowded the bedroom. They'd quarreled about it, with her complaining that they might as well have separate beds.

Kelsey frowned a little as the memories flickered across her mind. She couldn't remember ever waking up to find Rick on her side of the bed, let alone with his arm thrown over her.

She forced her eyelids to open and found herself staring into a pair of sleepy blue eyes. But not the pale, clear blue of Rick's eyes. These eyes were a deep, electric blue that seemed to look right inside her and see all the way to her soul.

Gage.

It was Gage's arm that lay across her stomach; Gage's body pressed against her side, the heat that radiated from him making her feel as if she were cuddled up to a furnace; Gage's hand that shifted, sliding upward to cup the rounded globe of her breast. Her nipple hardened instantly to the casual stroke of his thumb.

Gage.

She was still wrapped in sleep and a night's worth of loving, and her mouth curved with pleasure. It seemed the most natural thing in the world to be waking like this, to feel Gage's hand slide into her hair, tilting her mouth to his, his muscled chest a sensuous weight against her breasts.

Their kiss was long and slow and deep. It was followed by another and yet another until there was no beginning and no end, only the feel of Gage's mouth on hers, the solid beat of his heart against her breastbone, the slide of his hand along her pliant body. A warm, liquid heat began inside Kelsey, spreading outward until her entire body was warmed by it and even her toes tingled with awareness.

Somewhere she heard a warning bell, a suggestion that all was not as it should be. There was something nagging at her attention. But she shoved the thought away, willingly slipping deeper still under the sensual spell Gage was weaving around her—that they were weaving around each other. As far as she was concerned, there was only the two of them in all the world. Only the two of them.

"Kelsey?" The voice came from a long way away, the tone sharp with concern. "Are you here?"

She felt Gage's sudden stillness and knew he must have heard it, too, which eliminated the possibility that it was a figment of her imagination. He lifted his head and looked down at her, his eyes dilated with arousal, his breathing uneven.

"Kelsey? Is everything okay?" The voice was closer now. It was also immediately—horrifyingly—familiar.

"Marilyn," Kelsey whispered in shock.

"Rick's mother?" Gage couldn't have looked more appalled if she'd said it was the president. For a split second, they were frozen in place, their gazes locked in shared horror.

"Kelsey? The back door was unlocked. Are you all right?"

"Ohmigod! She's coming this way." Kelsey's fingers had been sliding through his hair. Suddenly, her hands were flat against his chest, shoving him away. "She's coming this way. Ohmigod!"

"It's okay. She won't come to the back of the house."

"Kelsey?" Marilyn's voice made it clear that she was on her way down the hallway. And once she stepped into the back hall, she'd have a clear view into Gage's room. They'd left the door conveniently open, so there was no possible way she could miss seeing them.

"The door's open. Ohmigod!"

Kelsey scrambled to find her robe and get it on. Behind her she was aware of Gage's throwing himself off the bed and diving for his jeans. At another time, she might have been amused by the sight of his hopping around on one foot while trying to shove the other foot through the leg of his pants. But she wasn't in the mood to appreciate the humor just then. She was too busy trying to tie the belt of her robe and smooth her tangled hair at the same time.

"Kelsey?" There was real concern in her mother-in-law's voice, but Kelsey took more notice of how frighteningly close she sounded.

She started for the door with the vague idea of running down the hallway and heading Marilyn off. She didn't know if Gage had the same idea or if he was going for the more immediate solution of slamming the door shut. Whichever it was, the two of them tangled in the doorway. Kelsey's foot caught on Gage's ankle. She gasped as she felt herself falling, but then his arms came around her, hard and strong, catching her up against his chest.

"Kelsey?" Marilyn Jackson's voice preceded her by only a moment. "Are you...?" Her words trailed off in a squeak of surprise as she stepped around the corner and caught sight of her daughter-in-law and her son's best friend.

Kelsey closed her eyes for a moment, aware that the position they were in was only marginally better than if they'd still been in bed together. It must have been obvious that they'd just climbed out of bed. Their state of undress made that clear even if nothing else did. She'd managed to get her robe on, but the collar was rolled under, the belt sloppily tied. And Gage wore nothing but a pair of jeans that were zipped but not buttoned. Not to mention the fact that his arms were wrapped around her.

There was no pretending that what had happened *hadn't* happened. Not that she was even sure she wanted to pretend it hadn't. At the moment, the only thing she was sure of was that she wanted more than anything in the world to disappear in a puff of smoke so that she wouldn't have to face the awkward scene that was about to ensue. When no divine intervention was forthcoming, she opened her eyes. For a moment, her glance met Gage's, but she looked away before she could judge what he might be thinking.

"I . . . I'm sorry," Marilyn stammered, sounding as if she'd just been poleaxed. "The cars were here. You didn't answer the bell. The back door was open. I thought something might be wrong.... I didn't mean . . . I'm sorry," she said again.

"No need to apologize," Kelsey said quietly. She pressed against Gage's chest, feeling an immediate sense of loss when he released her. "I guess I...didn't hear the bell." But she had heard it. That must have been what awakened her. "We were...ah...I was..." She let the words trail off, aware that it was perfectly obvious why she hadn't responded to the doorbell.

"I knocked," Marilyn said, sounding as embarrassed as Kelsey felt. "Bill called. Danny's plane was a little early. They're on their way home. I ... wanted to let you know. He tried to call you but no one answered the phone and the machine didn't pick up.''

At the mention of her son, Kelsey felt a wave of guilt so strong it almost knocked her to her knees. Danny was coming home today. How could she have forgotten that? My God, what if he'd walked in on her and Gage in bed together? What would that have done to him?

"I think we could all use some coffee," Gage said, speaking for the first time.

"I'll make some," Marilyn said quickly, sounding grateful to have something to do. She disappeared toward the front of the house, moving so fast she was nearly trotting. She left a thick silence behind.

Groping for something to say, Gage stared at Kelsey's profile. She was obviously upset. Hell, so was he. The Jackson house had been a second home to him during all the years he and Rick were friends. The only thing more embarrassing than having Marilyn Jackson catch him in a compromising position would be for his *own* mother to show up.

"Kelsey—"

"Don't." She cut him off before he even knew what he was going to say. "I can't believe this happened."

Gage didn't know if she was referring to Marilyn's poorly timed arrival or their spending the night together. He opened his mouth to ask, though he wasn't sure he'd like the answer, but Kelsey was speaking again.

"It was the doorbell that woke me," she said, talking as much to herself as to him. "Why didn't I realize what it was?"

"You were tired." He didn't need to point out why she'd been so tired. It had been almost four when they fell asleep the first time. And then he'd awakened her at dawn and they'd made slow, sweet love, taking time for all the soft touches and softer sighs they'd skipped the first time.

Kelsey flushed, and he knew she was remembering, too. But the memory didn't seem to bring her any pleasure. She shook her head, still intent on piecing together the exact sequence of events that had led up to the embarrassing scene with her mother-in-law, as if knowing what had happened might help her figure out what to do next.

"I was thinking about Rick," she muttered. She spoke more to herself than to him, but it seemed as if she'd shouted the words, so loudly did they reverberate in his head.

She'd been thinking about Rick? When? When she was making love with *him?* The thought hit him with the force of a blow to the gut. He literally felt the breath go out of him. If Kelsey had been less absorbed in her own tortured thoughts, she might have seen the shocked surprise in Gage's eyes. But she was wrestling with her own demons.

"I've got to talk to Marilyn," she said, shaking herself out of the tangled web of her thoughts.

"Don't you think we should do a little talking ourselves?" The startled look she gave him made him realize that his voice was harsher than he'd intended. He took a deep breath and forced himself to speak in a more level tone. "We didn't exactly take time to discuss any of this beforehand."

He'd wanted to remind her of the urgency they'd both felt the night before, wanted her to remember that he hadn't been the only one to feel that urgency. From the color that flooded her face, he'd succeeded.

"I know." She twisted her fingers in the sloppy bow at her waist. Gage found himself unreasonably glad to see her discomfort. It wasn't particularly generous of him, but he didn't want to be the only one feeling like hell right now.

"We'll talk later," Kelsey said, the words half a question. Her eyes slid in his direction, then darted away without making contact. "I need to talk to Marilyn now. And Danny is due home." She hesitated, and this time her eyes made contact with his. "I don't want him to know that we...that you and I..."

"I'm not likely to tell Danny that I spent the night in bed with his mother," Gage snapped, furious that she thought it necessary to say anything. "My God, Kelsey, who the hell do you think you're talking to?"

"I'm sorry," she said immediately. When there was no softening of the anger in his eyes, she reached out to touch his arm, pleading with him to understand. "Please, Gage. Don't be angry. I know you wouldn't say anything to upset Danny. I'm so rattled, I don't know what I'm saying."

Did you mean it when you said you were thinking about Rick? But he wouldn't ask her that, not when he wasn't sure he wanted to hear the answer.

"I'm really sorry," she said again.

"Fine." Not the most gracious of acceptances, but it was the best he could manage at the moment.

The thud of a cupboard door shutting in the kitchen reminded them that they weren't alone in the house. Kelsey jerked as if the sound had been a gunshot. "I've got to go," she muttered, and moved away without giving him a chance to respond.

Gage waited until she'd disappeared into her bedroom before turning back to his own room. He shut the door behind him, wondering if things might have turned out a little better if he'd shut it the night before. It would have served to give them an additional few moments of privacy. They could at least have greeted Marilyn fully dressed. Maybe it wouldn't have been so obvious that they'd just climbed out of the same bed.

But embarrassing as it had been, his main concern wasn't Marilyn's reaction to what had happened—it was Kelsey's.

I was thinking about Rick. Gage sank down on the edge of the bed and stared blankly at the wall opposite. Had she been thinking of Rick while they were making love? He could live with damned near anything but that. Of course, maybe she *should* have been thinking about Rick. Hell, maybe *he* should have given some thought to his dead friend before he jumped into bed with his wife.

"I was just about to pour the coffee," Marilyn said brightly as soon as Kelsey entered the kitchen. "Your timing is perfect."

Kelsey wished she could say the same about Marilyn's own timing. If she'd just come over a little later— She broke the thought off, her skin suddenly heating with the realization of what Marilyn would have interrupted if she *had* come in a few minutes later.

She sank into a chair and watched her mother-in-law open the cupboard and take out two cups. She saw the other woman's hand hesitate over a third mug, but the rush of water as a shower came on made it clear that Gage wasn't going to be joining them. Kelsey thought she detected an almost imperceptible easing of Marilyn's tension and spared a thought for the irony of the two of them sharing a moment of unspoken relief.

She'd rushed through a shower and dragged on jeans and a loose T-shirt, fragile armor with which to face the consequences of the night before. But despite her best efforts, she couldn't move fast enough to escape her thoughts. And all her thoughts had circled back to Gage. Running soap over her skin, she had been reminded of the callused rasp of Gage's hands moving over the same territory, making her tremble and moan. Jerking a brush through her hair, she'd suddenly thought of the way he'd threaded his fingers through it, his palms cupping her head to tilt her face toward his. From there, it was only a heartbeat away to remembering the feel of his mouth on hers.

As if to punish herself for those thoughts, she'd dragged her hair back, securing it with an elastic band at the base of her skull, wielding hairpins like weapons to ruthlessly secure any stray tendrils that attempted to escape confinement. But when she looked at her reflection, she'd been forced to admit that the severe hairstyle and lack of makeup couldn't conceal the almost luminous glow of her skin and the slightly languorous look in her eyes that spoke of a woman who'd been recently—and thoroughly—loved. Despairing, she'd left her room to confront her punishment in the form of facing her mother-in-law.

But Marilyn didn't seem interested in dealing out reproaches or stitching up hair shirts. She set the filled mugs on the table and settled herself into a chair across from Kelsey.

"Bill said that Danny had a good flight," she said as she pulled the sugar bowl toward her.

"Good." At another time, Kelsey would have begged for every detail of her son's trip. Right now she had other things on her mind.

"From what Bill said, he slept the whole way home and was full of energy when Bill met him at the airport."

"I really appreciate Bill picking him up," Kelsey said, making an effort to hold up her end of the conversation.

"He had to be in L.A. anyway," Marilyn said as she spooned sugar into her cup. "And you know how much he loves spending time with Danny. He's so much like Rick was at that age."

Her voice trailed off uneasily as if it had occurred to her that maybe this wasn't the best time to be mentioning Rick. There was an awkward little moment of silence between them. In the midst of it, the thud of the pipes as the shower was turned off was as clear as a pistol shot.

"It will be nice to see him again, won't it?" Marilyn said, the words bursting out of her. She put another spoonful of sugar in her cup.

"Wonderful," Kelsey agreed. Apparently it was up to her to bring up the topic they were both so carefully avoiding. If she didn't say anything, Marilyn obviously wasn't going to, either. Tempting as the idea was, she knew it wouldn't work. Better to bring it out in the open and deal with it.

She fought the urge to press a hand to the knot in her stomach and drew a deep breath. "About what you saw earlier..."

"You don't owe me any explanations," Marilyn said immediately. "It's none of my business."

"I appreciate you saying that but I know it upset you."

"What makes you think that?" Marilyn's tone was a marvel of lightness, her smile dazzling in its brilliance. She lifted her cup in an effort to show her lack of concern.

"Because you don't normally put six teaspoons of sugar in your coffee," Kelsey pointed out dryly as Marilyn took a swallow of coffee.

"Oh!" The older woman's face puckered in distaste. The cup hit the table with a solid thunk, her throat working as she forced down the syrupy brew. "Oh, my. Six?" she asked faintly.

"At least." Kelsey rose and picked up Marilyn's cup. Carrying it to the sink, she emptied it and rinsed it out before refilling it with fresh coffee. She set it down in front of the other woman and returned to her own chair.

"I think I'll just drink it black this time," Marilyn said when Kelsey nudged the sugar bowl in her direction.

Their eyes met across the table, and they were suddenly smiling at each other.

Kelsey felt some of the tension drain away. She was very fond of her mother-in-law. Marilyn and Bill Jackson were the antithesis of all the hoary old jokes about in-laws and the problems they caused. Because she and Rick had met and fallen in love while he was working in Minnesota, his parents hadn't met her until a few days before the wedding. But they'd welcomed her into their family as if they'd known her for years. After all these years, she considered them as much her family as her own parents. She didn't want anything to damage that closeness.

"I know you must be wondering about what you saw earlier," Kelsey said. She herself was wondering what she was going to say.

"It really isn't any of my business," Marilyn said again.

Kelsey supposed that was true. She didn't owe anyone an explanation, especially when she couldn't even explain to herself what had happened. But she couldn't shake the feeling that she had to say *something*.

"Gage and I ... We haven't ... I don't want you to think that anything ... I mean, last night was the first time. The *only* time," she added hastily.

"Kelsey." Marilyn reached across the table and caught Kelsey's hand in her own. "I never, ever, doubted your faithfulness to my son."

It was only when she heard it said out loud that Kelsey realized that was exactly what she had been afraid of. It had been gnawing at her from the moment she'd heard the other woman's voice. She felt tears of relief sting her eyes. "Thank you," she said shakily.

Marilyn squeezed her hand and then released it. When she spoke, her tone held a touch of wistfulness. "It was a bit of a shock to see ... to think of you with someone besides Rick. But I don't want you to live the rest of your life mourning him. You're a young woman, and I'd like nothing better than to see you find happiness again."

Kelsey stared at her in shock. Good grief, she was talking as if she and Gage actually had a relationship, which they did, of course, but not the one that Marilyn was ascribing to them. They were just good friends. Well, after last night, maybe she couldn't describe it that way anymore, but they weren't what Marilyn seemed to think they must be.

"Gage and I . . . We aren't . . . I mean, we're really just friends," she finished lamely.

Marilyn looked doubtful but she was kind enough not to comment. "Well, you certainly couldn't have a better friend." But she couldn't resist adding, "And if I were looking for someone who'd make a good stepfather for Danny, I can't think of anyone who'd be a better choice than Gage."

Kelsey stared at her, her mind reverberating with the shock of Marilyn's words. There was no mistaking the fact that she'd just been given Marilyn's blessing to marry Gage. The shock of it was more than she could absorb. She and Gage were friends not—

Not lovers?

"I love Rick," she said, speaking to reassure herself more than anything else.

"I know you do, dear. But life does move on, and he'd never have wanted you to stop living." It was fortunate that Marilyn didn't seem to expect a response, because Kelsey was utterly incapable of giving one.

"I suppose I ought to get going," Marilyn said, glancing at the clock that hung near the door. She took a sip of her coffee and grimaced at the taste of it unsweetened. "I'm sure you have a lot of things you want to do before Danny gets home. If you don't mind, I'll come back this evening to see him. I know it's only been two weeks, but I've missed him."

"No!"

Marilyn's neatly plucked eyebrows shot up so high, they nearly disappeared into her hairline. "You don't want me to come by?"

"No. I mean, yes. Of course you can come by. But wouldn't it be easier if you just stayed until Bill brings him home? I know Danny would love to see you."

"But don't you have...things to do?" Marilyn glanced significantly in the direction of the bedrooms.

"Nothing that can't wait," Kelsey said, forcing an unconcerned smile.

"Well, if you're sure. I really would like to see Danny."

"I'm sure," Kelsey assured her, thinking that the last thing she wanted right now was to be left alone with Gage. She needed a little time to think, time to figure out what to say to him.

"Then I'll stay." Marilyn smiled at her, relieved by this evidence that their relationship hadn't been damaged by the morning's surprises.

"Did you leave me any coffee?"

At the sound of Gage's voice, both women started. He stood in the doorway, freshly shaved, his dark hair damp from the shower. He looked like an ad for a man's cologne—something guaranteed to be lethal to any female within range.

"There's plenty," Marilyn said, recovering her balance before Kelsey.

Actually Kelsey thought it was possible that she'd never regain her sense of balance. Not when just the sight of Gage had her pulse rocketing. She was painfully aware of him as he walked behind her chair. He smelled of soap and shampoo—homey scents that had no business creating such a knot of awareness in the pit of her stomach.

She stared down into her coffee cup, listening to him move around the kitchen, getting out a cup, pouring a cup of coffee. Out the corner of her eye, she saw him lean one hip against the counter, settling into a comfortable slouch, hands cradled around his cup.

The kitchen suddenly seemed amazingly silent. Marilyn busied herself with adding a spoonful of sugar to her coffee, which had to be lukewarm by now. At another time, Kelsey might have been amused by the way she pushed the sugar bowl away after adding the one careful spoonful. The sound of her spoon clicking against the sides of her cup echoed in the big room.

With an effort, Kelsey lifted her gaze to Gage's face. He was watching her, and she felt her heart thump when their eyes met. She could read nothing in his expression. His gaze was hooded, his eyes a cool, unreadable blue. The moment stretched, hovered on the edge of confrontation, and then he glanced away.

"So what time do you figure Bill and Danny will get here?" He directed the question to Marilyn, his tone casual.

Kelsey barely heard the answer. She was suddenly wondering if she'd really done herself a favor by postponing her talk with Gage. Maybe time to think wasn't such a good idea after all.

Chapter 10

As it turned out, time to think was not a part of the day's agenda. Kelsey was shamelessly willing to use Marilyn as a shield, but having the other woman around also precluded any deep, contemplative moments. Like Kelsey's own mother, Marilyn could carry on a conversation with very little help. The difference between the two women was that Kelsey's mother frequently felt obligated to offer unsolicited advice on the way her daughter was managing her life. Marilyn felt no such urge. She simply liked to talk, as she herself freely admitted. Everything from the weather to politics to celebrity life-styles was grist for her conversational mill. Kelsey found the nonstop chatter oddly soothing. Marilyn's rattling commentary was so undemanding, so utterly normal, that it was almost possible to pretend that nothing in her world had changed.

It helped that as soon as he'd finished his coffee Gage disappeared outside to work on the greenhouse. Out of sight wasn't exactly out of mind, but at least she didn't have to cope with the erratic behavior of her own pulse whenever he was around. She was grateful when he didn't reappear again until Danny and Bill arrived.

Kelsey hurried out of the house as soon as she heard her father-in-law's car pull into the driveway. She saw Bill lean across the car to help Danny unlatch his seat belt, and then the passenger door was opening and Danny was hurtling toward her, a missile in jeans and striped T-shirt.

"Mama!" The excitement in his voice released the tenuous hold Kelsey had on her emotions. She dropped to her knees in the grass, feeling tears fill her eyes as she held out her arms to him.

"Baby!" Only he wasn't a baby anymore, she thought as he threw himself into her arms. It seemed as if in just two weeks he'd grown a ridiculous amount. Holding her son's sturdy little body, his arms around her neck as he planted a wet kiss on her cheek, Kelsey felt her world shift and settle into place. No matter what else happened, she had Danny to give her life balance and meaning. There was nothing else half so important as that.

But her newfound peace was shaken moments later when Gage walked around the side of the house. Danny had been chattering a mile a minute, apparently trying to tell his mother and grandmother everything that had happened every minute of the past two weeks. He was in the midst of a convoluted story that seemed to involve the neighbor's dog, his grandmother's cat and a great deal of hand waving when he saw Gage.

"Uncle Gage!" The story was forgotten as he shot across the yard, his short legs churning with excitement. He launched himself at Gage as if shot from a rocket.

"Hey, buddy!" Gage caught the boy easily, swinging him up into the air. "Good grief, what did they feed you? Lead pancakes? You must have gained twenty pounds." He pretended to stagger under the added weight, eliciting a peal of delighted laughter.

"I don't know where children get their energy," Marilyn commented, watching her grandson launch into yet another story.

"Batteries," Kelsey murmured. She was also watching Gage and Danny, but her expression was more thoughtful than indulgent.

Gage meant so much to Danny. Since Rick's death, he'd been the only real father figure Danny had. It had never seemed to matter that his visits home were months apart. When Gage was home, he and Danny were almost inseparable. He was listening to what Danny was saying with the same attention he'd have given an adult, despite the fact that, as near she could tell, the story was not particularly coherent. He bent his head attentively close to Danny's, his dark hair contrasting with her son's almost white, blond curls.

He was remarkably good with the boy, Kelsey thought, watching him settle the child on his hip. It was starting to sink in on her that sleeping with Gage the night before could have consequences beyond what she'd originally thought. She'd been worried about what might happen to her relationship with Gage, where they'd go from here. But there was more than just the two of them involved. Whatever had happened between them or might happen in the future, she couldn't let anything interfere with Danny's relationship with Gage. Her son had already lost too much in his short lifetime.

That thought lingered throughout the afternoon. She conversed with her in-laws, listened to Danny's apparently endless stream of stories about his trip, cooked dinner and even managed to act naturally around Gage. But always in the back of her mind was the knowledge that no matter what else, she was not going to see Danny hurt.

Danny's energy began to flag soon after dinner. Marilyn and Bill said their goodbyes after kissing their sleepy grandson good-night.

"Time for bed," Kelsey announced as the door closed behind them.

"I'm not tired," Danny protested automatically. But his drooping head suggested otherwise.

"And the Pope ain't Catholic," Gage murmured as he walked past Kelsey. "How about if I carry you to bed?" he suggested to Danny.

Tired enough to be feeling a little cranky, Danny thrust his lower lip out and hugged the corner of the sofa as if fearing to be wrenched away from his only hope of happiness. "I don't wanna go to bed," he whined. "I don't have to go to bed till nine. It's only eight."

Kelsey remembered how hard she'd worked to teach him to tell time and shook her head over her own stupidity. She stared at her son, reading the stubborn jut of his chin, the warning in his eyes. The last thing she wanted was to end the day with a major tantrum.

Maybe she could just let him stay up. He was sure to fall asleep in a few minutes anyway, and then she could put him to bed. But before she was forced to resort to such cowardly measures, she was struck by inspiration.

"You remember how it's a different time in different parts of the country, how we have to know what time it is where Granny and Granddad are before we call them?"

Danny nodded warily, perhaps sensing a trap beneath his mother's reasonable tone.

"Well, since you've been staying with them, your body is still on Minnesota time. And it's ten o'clock in Minnesota right now, so it's really an hour past your bedtime."

Danny hesitated, caught between a feeling that he was being cheated out of a whole hour of the day and the exhaustion tugging at him.

"You're a regular night owl," Gage said. "We'd better get you to bed before you turn into a pumpkin." He reached down and swung the boy up into his arms. "If you turn into a pumpkin, we'll have to put a candle in your mouth and set you on the porch for Halloween."

"People don't turn into punkins," Danny protested, but he put his arms around Gage's neck and let his head drop onto his shoulder.

"Even if you did, Halloween is so far off, you'd probably rot before then," Gage told him as he carried him out of the living room.

"Then Mom'd throw me on the compost pile." Danny's voice was slurred with sleep.

"She probably would." Gage nudged open Danny's bedroom door and carried him inside to lay him on the bed. He stepped back to allow Kelsey to sit on the edge of the bed and start undressing Danny, who was already half-asleep.

"Good night, buddy."

"'Night, Uncle Gage."

Gage watched Kelsey for a moment. All her attention seemed to be on Danny, but he didn't doubt that she knew exactly where he was. They'd been attuned to each other all day, like it or not. And it was pretty clear she *didn't* like it, he thought, noticing that her hands were not quite steady.

"I'll put on a pot of coffee," he told her.

She'd been in the process of slipping Danny's shoes off. At his words, she froze, reminding him of a doe caught in the glare of headlights. He waited for her to tell him that she was tired, that she was going to go straight to bed.

"Make it decaf," she said quietly as she slid Danny's sneaker off and set it on the floor beside the bed.

"Decaf," he said, setting her cup on the kitchen table a little while later. "Is he settled in?"

"Already out like a light." Kelsey wrapped her hands around the cup as if craving the warmth of it against her skin.

"Sounds like he had a good time with your parents," Gage said. He sank into a chair across from her, pretending not to see the uneasy glance she slanted him.

"From what my mom said when I talked to her, he ran them ragged."

"And they loved every minute of it."

"Adored it." One corner of her mouth kicked up in a half smile, the closest he'd been to getting a smile out of her all day. "It's good to have him home," she said.

"Yeah. I was starting to get bored with all that peace and quiet," Gage said dryly.

Kelsey's smile was even more faint this time. She moved her cup in tiny circles on the tabletop. "He loves you very much," she said, seeming to speak as much to herself as to him.

Gage said nothing. It didn't take a genius to figure out where she was going with this, but he'd let her finish. Maybe she'd surprise him.

"He's lost so much," she murmured, her eyes on the aimless movement of her cup.

He let the silence stretch until it became awkward. But what the hell *hadn't* been awkward between them today? She'd been jumpy as hell every time he got within fifty feet of her. Not that he'd been much better. Damn, how could things have changed so much in less than twenty-four hours?

"I take it you're worried that the fact you spent last night in my bed might affect my relationship with Danny," he said finally.

"He's lost too much already."

"Why should the fact that you and I are lovers mean that he'll lose me?" He saw her flinch at the deliberate intimacy of his tone. Something inside him tightened into a knot.

"We aren't—"

"Lovers?" he finished when she couldn't seem to get the word out. "I'd have to argue that one."

"Last night...what we did..." She stopped and closed her eyes for a moment, as if trying to gather her thoughts. "We didn't think anything through last night."

He couldn't argue with that. He hadn't been thinking at all. He'd been too wrapped up in the taste of her, the feel of her in his arms, to be thinking about anything else. He wished he could be sure Kelsey had felt the same. But he kept hearing her saying that she'd been thinking about Rick.

"But you've thought things through now?" he asked.

"I've tried to."

"And I take it you've come to some conclusion." Her eyes flickered to his face and then away. He could make this easier for her, he thought, but he wasn't in a particularly generous mood at the moment.

"I... think we should forget last night ever happened." Kelsey almost slurred the words together in her rush to get them said.

It was exactly what he'd been expecting, but Gage felt the knot in his gut cinch just a little tighter. She'd been building up to this all day. He'd seen it in the way she avoided meeting his eyes, in the fine tension that radiated from her whenever he got too close. It was as if she'd posted psychic No Trespassing signs.

Forget about last night? Pretend he'd never held her, never been inside her, never felt her body shudder under his? Easier to forget his own name.

"Why?" Stupid question, he thought immediately. He knew why. It was because she still loved Rick, still felt married to him. Not that she'd say as much.

"I think it's best," she said. When he didn't respond, she lifted her gaze from the table and met his eyes. "I don't want things to change between us, Gage."

Too late. Things already *had* changed. He wasn't sitting across the table from a woman who was his friend. He was sitting across the table from a woman he'd made love to, a woman he wanted to make love to again.

But he didn't say that to her. He couldn't. Not when she was looking at him like that, her eyes pleading with him to agree with her, to pretend that everything could just go on the way it had been.

"I'm not sure it's that easy," he said slowly. "You can't just wave a wand and make it go away."

"We can try. I don't want to lose you."

"You keep talking about people losing me," he snapped. He shoved his chair away from the table and stood. "I'm starting to feel like a misplaced shovel!" He took a half turn away and then spun back to pin her to her seat with angry blue eyes. "What do you think is going to happen? Do you think that now that we've slept together, I'm going to walk out on you and Danny? That I've been living here all this time as part of some elaborate plot to get you into my bed?"

"Of course not."

"Then why the hell do you keep acting like that's what I'm going to do? My God, Kelsey, don't you know me better than that?" He thrust his fingers through his hair, feeling the anger drain away, leaving behind a vast emptiness.

"I know you'd never walk away as long as Danny or I needed you," she said quietly. "But I can't help but worry about the way this could affect our relationship. You've been such a good friend to us, and I . . . don't think I could bear it if anything happened to change that friendship."

It's already changed. But he kept silent. If she didn't see that herself, then maybe he was wrong after all. Maybe it hadn't changed. Maybe last night had been nothing more than a bizarre detour in their lives. If she could spend the night in his bed and then look at him with those big gray eyes and tell him she didn't want anything to change...

Gage turned away from her and stared out the window. From here he could see one corner of the greenhouse. He stared at the curved line of the roof and wondered how the hell he was supposed to pretend he didn't remember what it was like to make love to Kelsey.

I was thinking of Rick.

"So you want to just pretend last night never happened?"

When Kelsey hesitated, he turned to look at her, wondering if she was finally starting to see how crazy this whole idea was.

"There's more than just the two of us to think of," she said at last. "I have to think about Danny. He has to come first."

"And you think our being lovers is going to damage his psyche?" He asked the question without sarcasm, but Kelsey flushed anyway.

"You're very important to him. I don't want what happened between us to get in the way of your relationship with him. You're the closest thing to a father that he has, Gage."

Gage felt as if she'd just punched him in the gut. *Father?* Not him. Not ever. That was one thing that hadn't changed in the past twenty-four hours.

"He knows who his father was," he protested.

"Rick isn't much more than just a name to him," Kelsey said sadly. "He says he remembers him but what he remembers is the stories we've told him about his father. You're the one who taught him to throw a ball."

"I'm hardly ever here." Gage felt as if he was in the middle of a mine field without a map. "He thinks of me as his uncle, not as his father."

"I didn't say he thought you were actually his father. I said he thinks of you as if you were his father. I don't want to risk my friendship with you but I won't risk what you have with Danny. He needs you too much. If you and I got involved and things didn't work out..." She let a shrug finish the sentence. "Danny's already lost too much."

Gage could have argued. He could have pointed out she was taking a pessimistic view of things, that there was no reason to assume that their relationship wouldn't work out or that they couldn't remain friends even if it didn't. There were a lot of things he could have said, but he didn't say any of them. Because of one simple, two-syllable word.

Father.

And he'd suddenly seen what she'd been trying to tell him all along. If they took their relationship to what seemed like the next obvious step, Danny might start to see him not just as an almost-father but as the genuine article, and that would not be a good idea.

He reached for his coffee cup, wrapping both hands around it, though there was little heat left in it. The thought of being the boy's godfather had scared him half to death, but he'd adjusted to the idea and even come to like it. Then Rick had died, and he'd found the responsibility considerably more hands-on than anyone had anticipated. And he'd done all right there, too. He loved Danny. Hell, who wouldn't love the kid? But that didn't make him a father. He'd known years ago that he had no business taking on that particular responsibility.

No, he was a pretty fair adoptive uncle but he couldn't let it go any further, not when he knew better than anyone just how badly he might fail the boy. The way he'd failed Shannon all those years ago.

Kelsey watched his face and wondered what he was thinking to bring such a bleak expression to his eyes. If she'd had any vague thought that Gage might embrace the idea of himself as Danny's father, it was gone now. There'd been something approaching revulsion in his eyes before he looked away.

"I wouldn't hurt Danny—or you—for the world," he said finally.

"I know that."

There was another long silence, and she wondered if it was only her imagination that made it seem to echo with loneliness.

"So we just pretend last night never happened?" he said slowly

"I think it might be best."

"Best. Yeah. Maybe you're right." He lifted his cup and downed the lukewarm coffee. When he lowered it, his eyes met hers across the table. "Wouldn't want to spoil a beautiful friendship," he said, his mouth twisting in a rueful smile.

"No." But Kelsey was suddenly less sure of her decision. What if— She shook her head. She couldn't take that chance.

* * *

Gage had never in his life been so grateful to see the end of his vacation. The past two weeks had been close enough to hell that he wouldn't have been surprised if his hair smelled of sulfur. He had no one to blame but himself, he thought as he stuffed the last of his clothes into his duffel bag. He'd known it would never work, known he couldn't just forget what had happened. He was lousy at playing pretend.

He jerked the zipper on the duffel closed and glanced around the room to see if he'd missed anything. He'd always liked this room. It had been Kelsey's idea to convert the unused side porch into a bedroom for him. He'd felt at home here, as much at home as he was anywhere. But for the past two weeks, every time he stepped into the room, he saw Kelsey. He saw her standing by the bed, her robe pooled at her feet, her slender body trembling with urgency as he touched her. He saw her lying across the bed, the spill of her gold hair across the pillow, her gray eyes all smoky with hunger.

"Dammit!" The whispered curse held a savagery that reflected his extreme frustration. One night. One lousy night and everything was changed. His life here had been stripped bare, exposed as nothing but a thin facade. He'd spent the past four years playing house, calling this place home, pretending to be a family man. He'd borrowed a piece of his best friend's life. Rick's son, Rick's house. Rick's wife.

"Dammit." But the word held more resignation than anger. He scooped the duffel up off the bed and turned toward the door. It was four in the morning. Cole would be here any minute to drive him to the airport—an act above and beyond the call of brotherly duty, he'd pointed out.

Gage had said his goodbyes to Danny the night before. The boy hadn't cried, but his arms had clung a little longer than usual when Gage hugged him goodnight. He'd lingered beside Danny's bed for a moment, aware that six months was practically a lifetime to a child. He was suddenly conscious of how much Danny would grow between now and the time he came home again, of how much he was going to miss seeing.

He'd turned away, angry at himself for thinking that way, angry with Kelsey for putting that word in his head. *Father.* Just by saying it, she'd changed things, as if the fact that they'd slept together hadn't changed them enough already.

Gage glanced at Danny's door as he walked down the hall but he resisted the urge to go inside. Kelsey usually got up to see him off. Hopefully she'd forego that ritual this morning. He was in no mood for long goodbyes. The sooner he was on his way, the better.

He swallowed a curse when he saw the kitchen light on and smelled the rich fragrance of coffee. He dropped his duffel in the entryway and walked slowly toward the kitchen. He didn't know what he was going to say to her, any more than he'd known what to say to her for the past two weeks.

He was racking his brain for some casual tidbit of conversation when he heard the low rumble of Cole's voice. The relief he felt undoubtedly marked him as a coward, but that didn't stop him from savoring it.

"I was going to throw ice water on your bed to wake you, but Kelsey wouldn't let me," Cole said by way of greeting.

"I'd hate to have to delay getting back to work to visit you in the hospital." Gage murmured his thanks to Kelsey when she handed him a cup of coffee.

"You don't scare me. Unless things have changed since we were kids, you're barely functional at this hour."

Unbidden, unwelcome, Gage's thoughts flashed to waking before dawn and making slow, thorough love to Kelsey. Without conscious thought, he looked at her, something he'd done his best to avoid lately. Their eyes met, clear blue tangling with smoky gray. He saw the color come up in her cheeks, saw the memory in her eyes and knew he wasn't the only one who hadn't been able to put that night from his mind.

Neither of them noticed Cole's dark eyes going from one to the other, noting the tension between them. His brows rose a little, and he looked away.

"I'm going to head out to the truck. Thanks for the coffee, Kelsey."

He was gone before either of them could muster a protest. He left behind a silence so profound that the quiet click of the front door closing behind him sounded like a rifle shot.

"I think he was giving us a chance to say goodbye in private," Gage said, contemplating the possibility of making Cole run alongside his own truck all the way to L.A.

"That's silly." Kelsey picked up a sponge and busied herself with wiping an invisible spot off the counter. "Why would he think we needed privacy to say goodbye?"

"I don't know." Gage gulped down the contents of his cup, welcoming the pain as the hot liquid scorched his throat. "Doesn't seem necessary when we're just good friends."

He saw Kelsey flinch at the bitter emphasis he put on the last three words and immediately regretted his tone. It wasn't as if this mess was her fault. She couldn't help it that she still loved Rick, couldn't change the fact that he'd be damned poor father-material even if she tried.

"Sorry," he muttered as he set his cup down on the table. "You know how to get hold of me if you need me."

"Yes."

They had the same conversation every time he left. She usually teased him about his insistence that she have every number he could think to give her. This morning there was not even a smile between them.

"I won't be back until sometime around the end of the year." He stared at her bent head, aware of an aching emptiness in his gut.

"Be careful," she said just as she always did. She lifted her gaze to his face, and Gage thought she looked like an angel, standing there in her plain white robe, with the light catching in her golden hair and her eyes solemn and a little uncertain.

Time apart was the best thing, he told himself. Time to forget, time to put things back on an even keel. After all, what was one night stacked up against all the years they'd known each other? Even if it had been the most incredible night he'd ever spent, even if the scent of her, the taste of her, was imprinted on his very soul. Six months was a long time. When he came home, everything would be back to normal.

"Ah, hell."

One long stride covered the distance between them, and he wrapped one hand around the back of Kelsey's neck. She gasped, her hand coming up to press against his chest. But the small protest, if that was what she'd intended, ended the moment his mouth closed over hers. Her fingers curled into the fabric of his shirt, clinging to him as he slowly, thoroughly ravaged her mouth.

Gage ended the kiss as abruptly as he'd begun it. Lifting his head, he stared down into Kelsey's face, seeing the color that had come up in her face and, when her lashes lifted, the dazed look in her eyes. He took a purely masculine pleasure in that look and in the fact that her fingers were wrapped in the fabric of his shirt.

In that moment, he knew that whatever lay in the future, they couldn't return to the past. His head filled with the soft feminine scent of her, he felt a surge of totally unfounded confidence. With work and time, they'd find a way to move forward.

"Friends be damned," he said.

He dropped another quick kiss on her mouth before striding from the kitchen, leaving her staring after him with dazed eyes.

Chapter 11

"You've been staring at your fish like you expect to find the answer to the meaning of life hidden under it. Is there something wrong with it?"

Clair's quizzical tone made Kelsey realize that she wasn't exactly holding up her end of the conversation. She forced a smile and made an effort to throw off her preoccupation.

"Sorry. I didn't mean to space out on you. The fish is fine. In fact, this is a terrific restaurant." The remark was a deliberate attempt to distract Clair from asking the questions Kelsey could see in her eyes. It worked like a charm.

"Anton's done a fantastic job with the place, hasn't he?"

Anton was the new man in Clair's life, a tall, lanky chef who, despite his name, had been born and raised in Cleveland. The restaurant was his brainchild, the menu a mixture of Tex-Mex and California cuisine that had drawn considerable praise for its innovative combinations. Personally Kelsey had never seen any reason to pair *habañero* chilies, raspberries and duck breast cooked rare, but she was willing to concede that maybe she spent too much time with a six-year-old who regarded anything unfamiliar on his plate with deep suspicion.

Kelsey listened as Clair quoted a few of the more noteworthy bits of praise that had been heaped on Anton—not to mention his duck breast. It was nice to see her old friend so happy and in love. She hoped Anton proved more worthy of that love than Clair's first husband. At least Anton didn't seem likely to have a portrait gallery to converse with. And she supposed true love could survive a few underdone duck breasts. Though, if it were her, the chili-and-raspberry stuff would have to go.

"I've been rattling on almost since we sat down." Clair fixed her with a bright, expectant look. "Tell me what's happening with you."

Kelsey stared at her while half a dozen possible replies flashed through her mind. She discarded each of them in turn. Clair wouldn't be interested in how the gardens were doing or the new restaurant that had called and asked if she could supply them with a fair percentage of their fresh vegetables. She made a mental note to speak to Anton, see if he would be interested in having her supply his restaurant, though she'd have to be careful not to ask what bizarre things he might plan to do to her carefully grown produce.

She could mention Danny's latest escapades but she knew that wasn't what Clair wanted to hear. When Clair asked what was happening with her, she meant only one thing: was there a man in Kelsey's life?

"Nothing," she said. She put a bite of fish in her mouth and tried to look as if she wanted to concentrate on her meal. What on earth was in the sauce that decorated the fish?

"Nothing?" Clair frowned in disapproval. "You're too young to have 'nothing' going on in your life, Kelsey. When was the last time you had a date?"

"College," Kelsey answered promptly. She grinned at Clair and debated whether or not to ask exactly what it was she was eating. If nothing else, it might serve to change the subject. The fish was a perfectly innocent piece of red snapper, but the sauce was definitely... unique. She took a sip of water to wash the taste out of her mouth.

"What about Gage?"

Kelsey felt her expression stiffen and made a deliberate effort to relax. "He started a new job two months ago and won't be home until sometime around the first of the year."

That was just the right tone, she congratulated herself. Exactly the tone you might expect someone to use when they were discussing a friend. Certainly nothing to make anyone suspect anything else.

"I still can't believe that you're living with a guy who's that gorgeous, not to mention that he's nice, and you're nothing but friends."

"Believe it."

"I do." Clair waved her fork in a gesture that was supposed to indicate her faith in Kelsey's veracity. "I believe you. I think you're nuts but I believe you. He's just too damned gorgeous to leave lying around unclaimed. I mean, is that even legal?"

Kelsey laughed as Clair had intended and hoped her friend wouldn't hear the hollow sound of it. It was nice that Clair believed her when she said there was nothing but friendship between Gage and herself. It was too bad that she was no longer quite so sure herself.

She considered that thought an hour later as she left the outskirts of Santa Barbara and headed the car north on Highway 101. Nothing but friends? She and Gage? Not exactly an accurate description anymore. Not after what had happened last time he was home. Not now that— But she wasn't going to think about that right now. She *couldn't* think about that right now. Not until she'd had time to let it sink in.

Two months, and all it took was Clair's mentioning his name to bring the memories tumbling back over her. She'd been a fool to think that things could ever go back to the way they had been. When she and Gage had made love, they'd crossed an invisible barrier, and there was no stepping back over it and forgetting what had happened. Not when two months later her skin still tingled at the thought of his touch.

But tingles or not, the situation hadn't really changed since he'd left. She ignored the small voice in her head that suggested it had changed a great deal. She still had to consider what was best. Not necessarily what she wanted most, but what was going to cause the least amount of damage to all their lives. She'd spent some long, sleepless nights, particularly this past week when it had been brought home to her that there could be no going back to what used to be. And out of all the uncertainty, she'd come to one solid conclusion: Gage couldn't be her "roommate" anymore.

It just wasn't going to work. She wanted—needed—him to stay a part of their lives, but they had to put things on a different footing. And that wasn't going to happen as long as he lived in the same house. She'd made the decision last night, in the wee hours of the morning. She'd shed a few tears afterward, but her conviction had remained. They couldn't put things right until he moved out. When she got home, she was going to write him a long letter explaining her thinking.

But when she got home, the message light on the answering machine was blinking. As always whenever Danny was out of her sight, she lived with the secret, niggling fear that something terrible might happen to him, so she dropped her purse on the table and jabbed her finger on the appropriate button even before she kicked off her shoes.

"Kelsey?"

She froze at the sound of Gage's voice. It sounded as if he were standing in the room with her, and she didn't have to close her eyes to picture his leaning against the counter, a wicked grin curling his mouth, his electric blue eyes laughing at her. And that lock of hair that always fell onto his forehead like a dark question mark and made her fingers itch to push it back.

She was so absorbed in the vision her mind had painted that she missed hearing his message and had to rewind the tape to play it again.

"I'm at LAX. I'll be home as soon as I can catch a ride. I know you're not expecting me." He was speaking slowly and carefully, as if he had to concentrate on each word. Kelsey frowned and bumped up the volume on the answering machine. "I'll explain when I get there. Just wanted to give you some warning." There was a pause, as if he'd thought about saying more. But if he had, he must have changed his mind and hung up instead.

Kelsey replayed the message twice, analyzing every word. What did he mean by "I'll explain when I get there"? Explain what? And why was he talking with such deliberation? But no matter how many times she played the tape, he didn't say anything else.

She hit the Reset button with an irritated punch of her finger. Looking at the clock, she did a quick calculation based on when he'd made the call and realized that, depending on how long it had taken him to arrange transportation, he could be here any minute.

Her heart thumped in sudden panic. She wasn't ready for this. Her expression grim, Kelsey headed for her bedroom. When in doubt, change clothes, she thought, unbuttoning her blouse as she went. At least Danny was with Marilyn and Bill for the afternoon. Thank heavens for small favors—she didn't have to worry about him when she talked to Gage. Because, whether by letter—which she'd much prefer—or face-to-face, she had to tell him the same thing: he had to move out.

What was she going to say to him? *Hello, Gage. Nice to see you and, by the way, you're evicted?*

She pulled open her closet doors and stared at the rack of clothing without seeing it. In her mind's eye, she could picture Gage's face, could see the shock in his eyes, the hurt. She couldn't do it. Kelsey braced one arm on the edge of the closet door and leaned her forehead against it, her eyes closed. She just couldn't do it. She couldn't look him in the eyes—those gorgeous blue eyes—and tell him she didn't want to share a house with him anymore.

You have to. Either that or tell him the truth. The thought was enough to make her shudder and close her eyes. She'd have to find the strength to ask him to leave. Unless— She brightened as a new thought occurred to her. Maybe he was only going to be here for a few days. If that was the case, then she could wait until after he'd gone back to South America and write him a letter just the way she'd planned. It was a coward's way out, but she wasn't too proud to take it.

Feeling as if she just might survive this new crisis, Kelsey changed into a pair of jeans and a hot pink T-shirt, hoping the bright color would bolster her courage. She brushed her hair, avoiding her reflection in the mirror as she did so. She already felt shaky enough without seeing the doubts she knew must be in her eyes.

Kelsey spent the next half hour getting Gage's room ready. Though he'd always insisted that he was perfectly capable of making a bed and could probably even wield a feather duster if he tried, she'd always put fresh sheets on his bed, dusted the room and checked to make sure that the bathroom he shared with Danny wasn't overstocked with action figures and bathtub-scale battleships.

It was a way of welcoming him home. In the past, she'd used the time to think of all the things she wanted to tell him—things Danny had said or done, what was happening in her business. But today all she could think of was how she was going to get through this visit and offer up prayers that it was a short one.

Once Gage's room was ready, Kelsey made a pot of coffee and then sat at the kitchen table, staring at nothing. There were any number of things she could have done. Between running a business and raising a

child, there was never a shortage of tasks to occupy an
idle moment. But she knew she wouldn't be able to
concentrate on anything, not with Gage about to ar-
rive, not when her stomach was in knots over what to
say to him.

It was almost a relief when she heard a car pull up
to the curb. A moment later, a door slammed and then
the car pulled away. Kelsey stayed right where she was,
her entire body rigid with tension as she waited for
Gage to walk into the house.

What was taking him so long? Was he trying *to torture her?* The last thought was so completely irra-
tional that she gave a choke of laughter and then
clamped one hand over her mouth, afraid she was on
the verge of hysteria. She dropped her hand and drew
a deep, slow breath. This was Gage she was waiting
for, not Charles Manson. There was no reason to be
nervous. It wasn't as if he could just look at her and
know anything, after all.

Was he crawling *up the damned walkway?*

Just when she thought the waiting would be the
death of her, she heard his footsteps on the porch. The
chime of the doorbell seemed loud as a trumpet blast.
Kelsey shot to her feet, her pulse beating much too
fast. Why was he ringing the doorbell? Had he lost his
key?

She hurried into the entryway and then hesitated
with her hand on the doorknob. What if she'd gone
through all this and it wasn't Gage? What if it was
some kid trying to sell her a magazine subscription so
he could win a trip to Walt Disney World? In the
mood she was in, she could probably give him a look
hot enough to blast him all the way to Florida.

"Kelsey?"

Well, that answered one question. It was definitely Gage. Kelsey drew a deep breath, stretched her mouth in a smile she hoped felt more natural than it looked and pulled open the door. But the smile vanished, and her rehearsed greeting went right along with it.

"Oh, my God! What happened?"

"I missed a step," he said lightly.

And that had to be the understatement of the year, Kelsey thought as she took stock of his injuries. One side of his face, from forehead to chin, was marked by nearly healed friction burns, and his right arm was in a sling.

"Must have been a hell of a step."

"Yeah." One corner of his mouth quirked in a halfhearted smile. "Think I could come in?"

"Of course." She stepped back from the door.

But he didn't immediately step inside. He stood in the doorway for a long moment, his left hand braced on the doorframe. Kelsey looked at him a little more closely, looking past the obvious injuries and seeing the gray tinge to his face, the haze of pain and exhaustion that dulled his blue eyes. She realized suddenly that he was holding himself upright with sheer willpower.

She was beside him in an instant, easing herself between him and the doorframe, getting her shoulder under his left arm, wrapping her arm around his waist.

"Lean on me."

"I'm too heavy." There was a slurred sound to his words that frightened her.

"If you pass out in the entryway, I'm going to drag you onto the porch and leave you there," she told him sharply. "Put your arm around me."

"I'm okay," he told her, but he was already obeying her.

"Can you make it as far as your room? Or shall we try for the sofa?"

"Sofa's too short. I'm okay."

"Sure you are." She didn't trouble to hide the skepticism in her voice. But he was right about the sofa. It wasn't long enough, or wide enough, for that matter. He'd be miserably uncomfortable, and it looked as if he had enough to make him uncomfortable without adding a too-short sofa to the list. Of course, if they couldn't make it to his bedroom, he wasn't going to be real comfortable on the floor in the hallway, either.

She realized almost immediately that he was in even worse shape than he looked, which was saying something. Besides the damage to his face and arm, he was favoring his right leg.

"Lean on me," she all but pleaded.

"Too heavy." The words seemed to take an enormous effort. "I'm okay," he said again, and she wondered if he thought repetition would make it a reality.

Willpower alone seemed to be keeping him upright. He allowed her to guide him but refused to put any of his weight on her shoulder. Kelsey didn't argue with him any further, concentrating instead on directing his footsteps, which showed an alarming tendency to weave. Questions nagged at her: What had happened? How badly was he hurt? But they'd have to wait. Right now the most important thing was to get him to bed before he passed out.

It was a step of less than two inches that caused the problem. Since Gage's bedroom had once been a porch, there was a shallow step down into it. It wasn't much but it was enough to throw off his already shaky balance. He tripped and, in trying to recover, brought his weight down solidly on his right leg. Kelsey heard him suck a sharp, pained breath between his teeth. She saw his eyes close and felt him sag against her and realized that he was going to black out.

"Don't you dare!"

She didn't know if he heard her or not, but at least he didn't collapse on the spot. Her one thought was to get him into the bed. Using every bit of strength she had, she shoved him in the right direction. Half dragging, half pushing, she bullied him the few feet necessary. She felt the bed come up against the back of her knees and saw Gage's eyes roll back in his head at the same instant. Wrapping her arms around him, she tugged him toward her, letting his weight carry her backward onto the mattress.

The bed frame creaked in protest at the impact of their combined weight. For several long moments, Kelsey didn't attempt to move, content to simply lie there and savor the relief of having gotten him here. Gage was sprawled half on top of her, his body a deadweight. It didn't take long for her lungs to protest the effort just to breathe, and she wiggled out from under him. Ten minutes later and more than a little winded, she had him lying on his back and had managed to get his boots off.

She stood beside the bed and watched him sleep. His breathing was deep and regular, and his color was a little better. She suspected that his condition was more a result of exhaustion than it was of his injuries.

What had happened to him? Why hadn't someone called to let her know that he was hurt? And how bad

were his injuries? He was lying so still. It was only
when she saw him like this that she realized she'd never
seen Gage in anything less than the peak of health,
never even seen him with a cold or flu.

Kelsey wrapped her arms around her waist, hugging herself against a sudden chill. It was frightening
to see him like this, to see him so vulnerable. It made
her realize how much she'd come to depend on his
strength. He'd always been there when she needed
him, solid as a rock, something she could hold on to
no matter what. Seeing him helpless shook her to the
core.

After checking his pulse one more time, she turned
and left the room. She was willing to bet that Gage
hadn't told his family that he'd been hurt, probably
hadn't even told them he was home yet. She'd call
Cole.

Chapter 12

Gage was aware of being watched even before he was sure he was awake. His first thought was that he was back in the hospital with a nurse hovering over him, about to poke him with one of the needles they wielded with merciless regularity. He stirred, thinking maybe he'd point out that he was tired of being treated like a pincushion. But when he opened his eyes, he didn't see the sterile whiteness of a hospital room but the soft gray blues of his own room.

He was home. The realization brought with it a wave of relief. He closed his eyes for a moment, savoring the feeling.

"No use closing your eyes. We're not going away."

At the sound of Cole's voice, Gage opened his eyes again, focusing on the small group of people standing at the foot of his bed. He blinked, and what had seemed at first to be a veritable crowd sorted itself into four people. Kelsey, his brother, Cole, and Cole's daughter, Mary, and Danny all regarded him with varying degrees of concern.

"What are you guys doing here? Am I dying?"

"Not immediately," Cole assured him.

"Considering the way I feel, I'm not so sure." Gage started to sit up and stopped when his rib cage issued a distinct warning. In deference to the children, he swallowed the short, pungent curse that rose to his lips but he couldn't prevent a pained gasp.

"Let me help." Kelsey was beside him in an instant, reaching for his shoulders.

"I don't need help," he said more sharply than he'd intended. He moderated his tone. "I'm okay."

She gave him the same look he'd seen her give Danny when the boy was being particularly unreasonable. "That's what you said right before you passed out," she told him with some asperity as she helped him sit up, stacking the pillows behind his back.

"I didn't pass out," he protested.

"You did a good imitation of it."

"Mama says you fell down, just like a big tree in the forest," Danny said. "You're not really going to die, are you, Uncle Gage?"

Gage saw the worry in his eyes and cursed his stupidity in joking about something that must be very real and frightening to Danny. He knew what death meant, more than any child his age should have to.

"Of course not." Ignoring the pain in his ribs, Gage hitched himself into a sitting position, leaning back against the pillows. He smiled, trying to look as if every bone in his body didn't ache. "I'm just a little banged up, that's all."

"You don't really want us to go away like Daddy said, do you, Uncle Gage?" That was Mary, her big brown eyes questioning. "You're glad we're here, aren't you?"

"Sure he is." Cole ruffled his daughter's fair hair. "Uncle Gage loves his family, don't you, bro?"

"Some members of it more than others," Gage said, shooting him a dark look. "I'm very glad you're here, Mary," he assured his niece.

"Did you fall down?" she asked, her dark eyes going over the scrape on his face and the sling on his arm.

"Yeah. I fell down big-time." Gage reached behind his neck, fumbling with the strap of the sling.

"You always were the clumsy one in the family," Cole said.

"Thanks for your tender concern," Gage said dryly. "Next time, Mary, leave your dad at home, okay?"

"I can't drive, Uncle Gage. I had to bring him." Her resigned tone made Gage laugh and then groan at the pain in his ribs.

"How sharper than a serpent's tooth," Cole said. "You're a rotten kid, Mary Elizabeth Walker. I'm going to have to teach you to show your respect for your elders." She giggled when he bent and scooped her up under his arm. He looked at Gage and Kelsey. "Excuse me while I go torture my daughter."

"Certainly." Kelsey nodded as if this were the most natural thing in the world. "When you're done, there's milk and cookies in the refrigerator. Why don't you show him where to find things, Danny?"

Danny looked uneasily at Cole, as if debating the possibility of torture. Mary's giggles seemed to reassure him that the threat wasn't to be taken too seriously, and his eyes shifted to Gage.

"I want to stay here," he said, edging closer to the bed. Obviously he was leery of letting Gage out of his sight. It wasn't hard to guess that he was thinking of his father.

"It's okay, buddy," Gage told him. "I'm not going anywhere."

Danny looked doubtful but he allowed himself to be persuaded and led the way out of Gage's room. The departure of Cole and the children left behind a deep silence. Gage looked at Kelsey.

"I passed out?"

"Like a light."

"Sorry about that." He reached back and tried to get hold of the strap again.

"What are you trying to do?"

"I'm trying to get this damned sling off," he snapped. "What does it look like I'm doing?"

A taut silence followed his words, and he didn't need to look at Kelsey to know he'd upset her. "Damn," he said softly. "I'm sorry, Kelsey. I didn't mean to snarl at you."

"I suppose if I offered to help, you'd tear my head off," Kelsey said tartly.

"I'd appreciate some help even if I don't deserve it."

"No, you don't." But she was already leaning over the bed. "Tilt your head forward."

Gage felt the brush of her fingers against the back of his neck. She braced one knee on the bed to get close enough to see what she was doing. She smelled of soap and shampoo and coffee, and he had to close his eyes against the urge to put his arms around her and pull her close to him.

Of course, he only had the full use of one arm, and his ribs would scream bloody murder if he made any hasty moves. Not to mention the fact that Kelsey might do the same, figuratively speaking, anyway. When he'd left two months ago, she'd been determined to turn back the clock and forget the one incredible night they'd spent together. In this very bed, he thought, aware that all he had to do was turn his head and his mouth would be almost touching her breast. And maybe then he could add missing teeth to his list of injuries, he thought ruefully.

"There." Kelsey eased the strap over his head. "What did you do to your arm?"

"I dislocated my shoulder." Gage used his good hand to strip the sling away, letting his arm rest against his stomach.

"And your face?" Kelsey was still half kneeling on the bed beside him. She reached out, tracing the scraped area with gentle fingers. Gage had to resist the urge to lean into her touch.

"I slid halfway down a mountain," he said lightly.

"On your face?" Cole's sardonic inquiry broke the fragile moment as effectively as a hammer striking a bone-china teacup.

Kelsey withdrew immediately, sliding her knee off the bed and bending to smooth the indentation it had left with quick, nervous movements. Gage gave his brother a look fierce enough to send a more sensitive man into a hasty retreat. Cole merely lifted his eyebrows and gave him a crooked—unrepentant, damn him—grin. He sauntered farther into the room.

"I left Danny and Mary feasting on cookies and milk and discussing the current political situation. So, what were you doing sliding down a mountain on your face?"

Forced to accept that fact that he wasn't going to get any more time alone with Kelsey—at least not right away—Gage gave in to the inevitable but not without another annoyed look in his brother's direction.

"There's not a whole lot to tell. We were in the middle of a torrential downpour, and I was trying to get some equipment under cover. I was standing at the top of a slope and lost my footing. I friction-burned my face, cracked a couple of ribs when I hit the bottom and dislocated my shoulder." If it wouldn't have been so painful, he would have dismissed his injuries with a shrug.

"You were favoring your right leg earlier," Kelsey said.

"What did you do to your leg?" There was a sharp note in Cole's question that belied his casual attitude.

"I caught it on a broken branch and did some damage," Gage admitted reluctantly. Hell, he was starting to sound like an invalid—a clumsy invalid. "I'm okay."

He caught Kelsey's look and amended it slightly. "I'm mostly okay. They wouldn't have sent me home except I ended up with an infection and spent a little time in the hospital, and they figured I'd better take some time to recuperate."

No need to mention that the branch had torn a jagged hole in his leg—which had taken more stitches to repair than he could count—or that the infection had proved resistant to antibiotics and there'd been a day or two where the doctors hadn't been too sure of keeping him alive. Even with what he'd said, Kelsey's face had drained of color, and her eyes had turned dull gray with fear.

"Hey, it's over and done, and I'm practically well again," Gage said, trying to reassure her.

"I'm going to go check on the children," she said, her voice thin and strained.

She was gone before Gage could say anything more. With a muttered curse, he moved to get off the bed.

"Let her go," Cole said. He came to sit on the edge of the bed, effectively blocking his brother's attempt to get up.

"She's upset."

"She just needs a couple of minutes to gather herself."

"Since when did you become such an expert on what Kelsey needs?" Gage snapped. If he hadn't been so damned sore, he'd have shoved Cole out of the way and gone after Kelsey. But despite his protestations, he was still weak as a kitten. And Cole knew it, damn him.

"I don't have to be an expert on Kelsey. I just have to use a little common sense," Cole said with a pointed glance. "This is probably a little too reminiscent of losing Rick. She'll be okay once she gets it through her head that you're not dead."

"I hadn't stopped to think that seeing me like this might remind her and Danny of what happened to Rick," Gage said slowly. "It was stupid to come here."

"They'll be fine. Of course, it doesn't help matters that you look like one of Freddy Krueger's victims," he added, narrowing his gaze on Gage's scraped face.

"Thanks, little brother. It's nice to know I can count on you to reassure me."

"You're welcome," Cole said. He was still grinning, but his dark eyes were sharp with concern when he continued. "How bad was it?"

Gage hesitated a moment and then answered honestly. "It wasn't good. But the damage isn't permanent." He shook his head, his mouth twisting in a rueful smile. "The hell of it was that I was supposed to leave for home the next day."

"I thought you weren't coming back until Christmas."

"I changed my plans." Gage's eyes drifted to the doorway through which Kelsey had disappeared.

"Have you told her you love her?" Cole's casual question snapped his brother's eyes back to his face. He met Gage's startled look calmly. "I know you pretty well," he pointed out.

"Not well enough," Gage muttered. "I'm not in love with her."

"Yeah, right. Have you told her?"

"Mind your own business."

"I didn't think so. What are you waiting for, an engraved invitation?"

"Who the hell died and made you Ann Landers?" Gage snarled. He would have given a great deal to be able to get up and walk away from this conversation, but getting up was a slow and painful process at the moment, which meant he was stuck.

"Just a piece of friendly advice." Cole was unperturbed by his brother's irritation. "Life's short. Don't waste it."

"Now you're talking like a saying on a T-shirt."

"Hey, there's some real wisdom to be found on T-shirts," Cole protested. "You don't get much deeper than 'Beam me up, Scotty. There's no intelligent life down here.'"

"You should certainly know," Gage muttered.

"If I didn't know better, I'd think you were trying to insult me."

"Maybe you're not as dumb as I thought."

"I suppose I'm too old to say 'It takes one to know one.'" Cole said thoughtfully.

Gage's laugh was reluctant and ended on a pained groan when his ribs protested. "I don't know why I didn't strangle you when we were kids."

"Because Mom would have given you one of her looks," Cole suggested.

"Mom. Does she know I'm one of the walking wounded?"

"More like the falling wounded," Cole said, unable to resist the jab. He shook his head in answer to Gage's question. "I haven't talked to her yet. She's spending the week in L.A. with Sam and Nikki. I figured I'd see just how desperate the situation was before dragging her home early. She claimed she wanted to do some shopping and go to the theater, but I think her visit had more to do with Jason Drummond than a sudden desire to see *Phantom of the Opera.*"

The brothers exchanged amused glances. Rachel Walker seemed to think that her four sons were oblivious to the fact that she and Jason Drummond were dating. It had been Nikki who'd introduced the courtly older man into her mother-in-law's life. He was Nikki's attorney, but it was as a friend of the family that he'd joined the Walkers for Thanksgiving the year before. Since then, he'd found a remarkable number of reasons to visit the little town of Los Olivos, and Rachel had been seized by a sudden fondness for Los Angeles.

"How long do you figure before he asks her to marry him?" Gage asked.

"Christmas."

"Ten bucks say he asks by Thanksgiving."

"You're on."

Grinning, they shook on it, and then Cole stood. "I'm going to gather up Mary and head home. I've got an early flight tomorrow morning, delivering some computer equipment to Sacramento." Cole was owner, operator and sole pilot of an air delivery service.

"Business is good?"

"I've got all I can handle. I'm even thinking about taking on a partner."

"Congratulations." Gage's smile faded, and he nodded toward the front of the house. "Mary's looking good."

"Yeah." Cole's eyes darkened with concern when he thought about his small daughter. "The doctor says she's doing okay, but they don't want to do surgery yet."

"He'll tell you when the time is right. She's getting the best care."

"That's what I keep telling myself, but it's not easy. I want her to be able to run and play like other kids her age."

"She will."

"Sure." With an effort, Cole shook off his pensive mood and focused on his older brother. "Get some rest. You look like hell."

"Thanks."

"Anytime." Cole lifted his hand in farewell and left Gage alone but with plenty to occupy his thoughts.

Kelsey turned the heat on under the pot she'd just set on the stove, adjusting the flame to high. She'd decided to make a pot of chicken soup. Never mind that it was September and the air-conditioning was working overtime to keep the house cool and that most sane people would have been thinking in terms of cool salads or possibly takeout. Gage needed nourishing food, and chicken soup seemed the only possible choice.

Behind her at the table, Danny and Mary were getting acquainted, their conversation leapfrogging from one topic to another in a way that made her head spin. What did that say about her, she wondered. When she couldn't follow a conversation that a pair of six-year-olds found perfectly coherent. Of course, at the moment she was having a hard time remembering her own name.

She had to keep struggling against the urge to run back to Gage's room and reassure herself that he was alive and well. As soon as she'd left his room, she'd felt the need to go back. If she could, she'd have pulled a chair up next to his bed and just sat there, staring at the rise and fall of his chest.

Ridiculous. She twisted the top off a spice jar and tossed a couple of bay leaves into the water with the chicken. Gage had been hurt but he was recovering. Her fears were not only unnecessary, but they were stupid. He wasn't going to die.

Rick had died. The insidious little whisper sent a shiver down her spine.

The situation was entirely different, she argued with herself. Rick had died instantly. He'd never had a chance. But Gage was getting better.

Determined to shake off her fear, she put a lid on the soup-to-be and turned to focus her attention on the children. Danny was talking a mile a minute, telling Mary about the tree house Gage had built for him. From his descriptions and grandiose arm gestures, he seemed to be describing a palace in the clouds. Kelsey bit her lip to hold back a smile. She lifted her eyes and saw Cole standing in the doorway, his eyes bright with laughter as he listened to Danny's description grow ever more remarkable.

"Sounds neat," Mary said when he finished, a piece of understatement to which Danny took immediate offense.

"It's the best tree house ever," he asserted fiercely. "Come on, I'll show you." He slid off his chair and started for the back door.

Mary looked up and saw her father. "Can I, Daddy?"

Cole glanced at Kelsey and, when she offered no objection, he nodded. "Make it a short visit, kiddo. We need to get home soon."

"I'll race you to the tree," Danny said as Mary slid off her chair.

"I can't," she told him. "I'm not supposed to run a lot 'cause there's a hole in my heart."

Kelsey sucked in a quick, shocked breath, her eyes jerking to Cole. His face twisted in sharp pain. It seemed to Kelsey as if the air was suddenly thick with tension, but the children were oblivious to it. There was a short pause while Danny absorbed this news about his new acquaintance.

"You really got a hole in your heart?" he asked.

"Uh-huh." She nodded, evincing no particular concern. "The doctors are goin' to patch it someday, but I gotta wait till I'm older."

"Neat," Danny said, and there was no mistaking the envy in his voice. "We can walk to the tree."

They disappeared out the back door, and Kelsey released her breath on a sound that hovered close to tears.

"Neat?" Cole said as he came into the kitchen. He shook his head, and she noticed that his eyes seemed a little too bright. "Out of the mouths of babes, huh?"

"Children see things differently."

"Thank God," he said fervently.

"I didn't know about Mary." Without asking, Kelsey got out a cup and poured him some coffee. He took it with a murmur of gratitude. "Gage never said anything."

"Maybe he thought I'd already told you."

"Is she . . . She mentioned some kind of patch?"

"I think she pictures it like a patch on a bicycle tire," Cole said with a choked laugh.

"She's going to be all right, isn't she?" Anything else was unthinkable.

"The odds are in her favor. It's a fairly common procedure. When she's older, when her heart is big enough, they'll repair the damage, and she should be like any other kid."

"It must be terrible for you." She was conscious of a rush of gratitude that Danny was healthy.

"I try not to think about it too much," Cole said. "It helps that it doesn't cause her too many problems."

"Well, it's certainly cemented her place in Danny's affections. I wouldn't be surprised if he asks me how come he doesn't have anything that 'neat,'" Kelsey said.

Their laughter cleared away the vague melancholy that had invaded the room.

"Too bad adults don't see things the way children do," Cole said, still chuckling.

"It would make life simpler, wouldn't it?"

"Speaking of making life simple, can you manage my lump of a brother on your own? He's going to make a lousy patient."

Kelsey stiffened at the mention of Gage, reminded of the myriad of problems his presence created. Obviously she couldn't ask him to move out now. Despite his insistence that he was fine, he obviously wasn't. He'd have to stay here until he healed, and there was no telling how long that would be. It could be weeks, which created its own set of worries. If he was here too long, he'd surely notice—

"Kelsey?" Cole's voice snapped her out of her thoughts. She drew a deep breath and gave him a quick smile.

"Sorry. I was just thinking about what Gage might need."

"If it's too much for you to take on, we can move him home. Mom would probably love a chance to fuss over one of us again."

"It's not too much. It's not like he's bedridden. I don't think he needs anything except someone to keep an eye on him and make sure he doesn't try to leap any tall buildings in a single bound. At least not for a week or two."

"He'll probably be a lousy patient," Cole warned her again.

"I'll manage." She gave him a smile filled with confidence.

"If you're sure."

"I'm sure."

If only she were half as sure as she sounded. She didn't doubt that she could handle whatever nursing Gage was likely to need—or to allow. Her concerns were more fundamental. Living in the same house, how long would it be before Gage began to suspect the truth?

How long before he realized she was pregnant with his child?

Chapter 13

"I'd never realized that falling down a mountain would cause such an outpouring of family feeling," Gage said as he limped back into the kitchen after seeing his brother Sam and his wife on their way back to Pasadena. "I didn't get this much attention when I was in the hospital."

"They're worried about you," Kelsey said.

"They don't have to be anymore. I'm practically good as new." He sank down on one of the kitchen chairs.

"Yeah, right." Kelsey gave a pointed glance at his injured leg, which he'd stretched out in front of him, and at his arm, which he was still favoring, though he'd left off the sling two days ago. "You're a hundred percent all right."

"Okay, so maybe I'm not completely back to normal," he conceded. "But I'm getting there. I'm not at death's door, and there's no reason for Sam and Nikki to drive up from L.A. to confirm it. And Keefe drove half the night to get here and then drove back the same day."

"They're your family. They love you. Would you rather they just ignored the fact that you've been hurt?" Kelsey hands moved quickly over the tomatoes that covered the counter, sorting them into separate piles by some criteria known only to her.

"Isn't there a happy medium between expressing concern and hovering? My mother has been here five times since I got back a little over a week ago."

"I like your mother," Kelsey said. She picked up a tomato, examined it briefly and then set it in the appropriate place.

"I like my mother, too. But she's got to stop treating me like she expects me to expire at any moment."

"She's your mother. She's supposed to worry. It's part of her job description." She glanced over her shoulder, her eyes meeting his for an instant before she turned her attention back to the tomatoes.

"Well, between her and my brothers, I'm starting to feel like Rick may have been right, after all—there is something to be said for being an only child."

He'd mentioned Rick deliberately and felt a certain bleak satisfaction when he saw the slight stiffening of her shoulders.

If there was anything good to come out of the hours he'd spent in bed since the fall, it was that it had given him plenty of time to think. And the thing he'd thought most about was Kelsey. It had taken him less than a month back at work to realize the absurdity of thinking that six months apart was going to make it possible for them to forget the night they'd spend together. The only way that was going to happen was if

they could make time run backward and erase that
night completely. And since that wasn't going to happen, they were going to have to find another way to
deal with it. It had taken him two weeks and the calling in of a lot of favors to arrange for more time off,
and then he'd fallen down the side of a mountain and
delayed his return still more.

When he'd finally made it home, he'd been weaker
than he'd expected and he'd spent most of the first
couple of days sleeping, telling himself that they'd talk
as soon as he got a little of his strength back. But he'd
been up and about for a good week now and they still
hadn't talked. Kelsey had done a remarkable job of
keeping a subtle distance between them.

On the surface, nothing had changed. She was
friendly. They spoke to each other. They even laughed
occasionally. But he'd noticed that she was careful to
steer the conversation away from anything remotely
personal. If the conversation showed any sign of
veering away from the safe and narrow, she suddenly
realized she had something urgent to do elsewhere.

Gage hadn't pressed her, thinking that, given a little time, she'd stop jumping every time he walked into
a room, stop finding things to do anywhere he wasn't,
stop talking to him as if he were a casual acquaintance rather than someone with whom she shared several years of friendship, not to mention one incredible
night in bed. But it had been over a week now, and his
patience was wearing thin. Maybe it was time to take
more positive action.

"What are you doing with these?"

At the sound of Gage's voice coming from right
behind her, Kelsey started, feeling her pulse suddenly
kick into high gear. After the comment about Rick,

he'd been quiet so long that she'd almost managed to forget he was there. No, that wasn't true—she hadn't forgotten. She hadn't been able to forget him for so much as a second since he'd come home. Come to think of it, the words *out of sight, out of mind* hadn't exactly applied even when he was gone, either.

"They're tomatoes. I'm sorting them," she said. It was difficult to force the words out past the sudden dryness of her throat.

"I may not be a farmer but I did recognize that they were tomatoes and I kind of guessed that you were sorting them. The question is—*why* are you sorting them?"

His tone was gently teasing. Kelsey felt a subtle loosening of the tension in her stomach. Despite herself, a smile tugged at the corner of her mouth.

"I wasn't sure you'd know what they were if they weren't already in a can."

"Don't malign my character. Just because I spent my formative years in Los Angeles instead of small-town Minnesota, that doesn't mean I don't know what a tomato is. They come in plastic bags from the supermarket. Everyone knows that."

His exaggerated tone of superiority made Kelsey's smile widen.

"How do you think they get into those plastic bags at the supermarket?" she asked, her fingers moving quickly over the mounds of bright red fruit, sorting out those with blemishes.

"The produce manager puts them there."

"And where do you think the produce manager gets the tomatoes to put in the bags?"

"That's easy." He picked up a tomato and tossed it idly in one hand. "They're stamped out of a factory somewhere in Idaho."

"They just taste like they're factory made. But somebody has to actually grow them."

"Like, in dirt?" He sounded so appalled that she bit her lip to hold back a smile. Casting him a stern look, she took the tomato from him and set it back on the counter.

"It's not dirt. It's soil," she corrected primly.

"How come it's soil when it's outside but dirt when it's on the floor?"

"It just is."

"Sounds like a blatant case of prejudice to me. Maybe we should find a lawyer to fight for more equitable treatment. We could come up with a slogan. Soil Forever, or Soil Isn't Dirty."

"I think you might have a hard time getting that campaign off the ground."

"I like a challenge. I managed to get you to look at me. I figure that proves it."

The brief moment of humor burst like a pinpricked balloon. Kelsey concentrated fiercely on the tomatoes. "I don't know what you mean."

"Sure, you do. You've been avoiding looking at me for a solid week." Gage leaned one hip against the counter and crossed his arms over his chest. He was much too close, much too large and much too masculine. "Afraid you'll turn to salt if you look at me, Kelsey?"

There was no mistaking the soft challenge in his voice, no ignoring the gauntlet that had been ever so lightly thrown down. Kelsey could feel his eyes on her, watching, waiting. She drew a deep breath and forced herself to look at him directly.

"There. I'm looking at you." The words didn't come out cool and confident, the way she'd intended. But she ignored the breathless uncertainty and lifted her chin a notch. "I haven't turned to salt so far."

"That's a start."

It took all her willpower not to look away from the searching blue of his gaze. It felt as if he were looking inside her, pulling out all her secrets. The thought of those secrets was enough to make her lower her eyes. This was one challenge she couldn't afford to accept.

"We need to talk, Kelsey." Gage's voice was gentle, but there was no mistaking the determination there.

"We talked before you left." She wasn't going to pretend that she didn't know what he meant but neither was she going to willingly open the subject again. Not here, not now.

"It's not going to work. This pretending that everything can just go back to the way it was. There've been too many changes."

More than you could possibly imagine. If he knew about the baby...

"We agreed—"

"We were idiots. We can't just pretend that night never happened. At least I can't. And if you could, you wouldn't be so nervous around me."

"I'm not nervous," she lied weakly. "Besides, we agreed this was the best way to handle things."

"Neither one of us was thinking clearly."

"Danny—"

"Danny isn't the problem right now." He reached out and cupped his hand around her chin, turning her

face up to his. Kelsey stiffened at the touch but she
didn't pull away. She forced herself to meet his gaze
without flinching.

"I want what's best for Danny, too," Gage said.
"But we can't keep up this pretense. It's not going to
work."

"I don't see why not."

"Because of this," he said, and lowered his mouth
to hers.

Afterward Kelsey was forced to admit to herself that
he'd given her more than enough time to pull away.
There was never a question of his forcing the kiss on
her, a consideration that she found almost harder to
forgive than the kiss itself. He didn't force her to hold
still, any more than he forced her mouth to open for
his or her hands to lift, her fingers curling into the
solid muscles of his shoulders.

Though she didn't remember turning toward him,
her body was suddenly curving into his. She heard him
groan, and then his arms were around her. Her breasts
were crushed against the width of his chest. He widened his stance, drawing her closer so that she was
pressed against the full length of his body.

It wasn't fair of him to remind her, she thought despairingly, not fair for him to make her remember, to
make her feel. She'd tried so hard to convince herself
that she'd forgotten what it felt like to have Gage
holding her, to feel the solid thump of his heart beneath her fingers, the warmth of his mouth against
hers.

She didn't know how long they stood there wrapped
in each other's arms. Long enough for her to remember how right it had felt to have him hold her, to have
him love her. Long enough for her fragile defenses to

come crashing down, leaving her achingly vulnerable and half-frightened by the need he created in her.

"My bike's got a flat tire, Uncle Gage. Can you fix it?"

Danny's voice preceded him by mere seconds. Long enough for Gage to break off the kiss, not long enough for Kelsey to step away from him. Not that she had much confidence in the ability of her knees to support her on their own. Her heart thumping with sudden panic, she turned her head to look at her son, aware that Gage was doing the same.

Danny had skidded to a halt in the kitchen doorway and was staring at the two of them, his eyes round with surprise and full of questions. Questions she couldn't even begin to answer, Kelsey realized despairingly. How was she supposed to explain to him why she was wrapped in Gage's arms when she couldn't even explain it to herself?

"Danny..."

Gage's voice overrode her apologetic beginning. "I think I can handle a flat tire," he told the boy. His tone was so casual that Kelsey shot him a look of disbelief as he released her. "Why don't you bring your bike around back and I'll take a look at it."

Danny hesitated a moment, looking from Gage to his mother. Kelsey felt the uncertainty in his look like a knife through her heart. She wanted to drop to her knees and hold her arms out to him, to beg his forgiveness. But Gage's response had given her a moment to think, and she knew he was right. The best way to handle this was casually. If she didn't make a big deal out of it, it wouldn't be a big deal to Danny.

Gage limped toward him. "Come on, buddy. Let's go take a look at your bike. Bet it's not as gimpy as I

am, is it?'' He held out his hand, and Danny took it
without hesitation.

"What's 'gimpy,' Uncle Gage?"

" 'Gimpy' is what happens when you're dumb
enough to fall down a mountain,'' Gage told him,
gesturing to his injured leg.

"You're not dumb, Uncle Gage. I think you're the
smartest guy in the whole world.'' The adoration in his
small face broke Kelsey's heart all over again.

"Thanks, kiddo. But I think you're biased.'' Gage
reached out to ruffle his fair hair, grinning down at the
small boy. "Take me to this wounded bike of yours.''

He turned his head before they went out the door,
his eyes meeting Kelsey's.

"We can't go back, Kelsey. We can only go forward.''

She watched the two of them leave and wondered
how two simple sentences could sound so threatening.

Over the years, it had become part of Danny's bedtime ritual that Gage spend a few minutes with him
before Kelsey came to tuck him in. Sometimes Gage
read him a story. Sometimes, they talked about whatever had happened during the day that Danny thought
warranted discussion. Gage enjoyed the ritual as much
as Danny did. It was a rare chance to see the world
through a child's eyes.

"Were you kissing Mama this afternoon?"

Gage had spent the afternoon half expecting the
question, but expecting it didn't mean he had an answer ready. The one thing he was sure of was that it
would be a mistake to lie about it.

"Yes, I was,'' he answered calmly.

"How come?"

The eternal question, Gage thought, amused despite himself. How should he answer? He chose an abbreviated version of the truth.

"Because I wanted to kiss her."

While Danny considered that, Gage sank down on the edge of his bed. He twisted so that he faced Danny, who sat cross-legged at the head of bed, his fair hair neatly combed, his face thoroughly washed, a cherub in Superman pajamas, Gage thought, half smiling. But Danny's next question made his smile vanish abruptly.

"Does that mean you're going to be my new dad?"

Gage stared at him, feeling as if he'd just taken a sharp blow to the solar plexus.

"What makes you think that?" he asked when he'd managed to regain his breath.

"'Cause when I was at Billy Desmond's house, his mom and dad were kissing and he said they do that all the time and that's how come he's got two little sisters. So I thought, if you were kissing Mama, maybe you were going to be my dad now." He shrugged and looked away, as if to say that it really didn't matter one way or another, but Gage wasn't fooled.

He'd been older than Danny when his own father was shot while trying to stop a liquor store robbery. He didn't know if having more memories had made it easier for him or harder. But he knew the hunger Danny was feeling, the empty space in the boy's life.

How the hell was he supposed to answer his question when he didn't even know what was going on between him and Kelsey? A few weeks ago, he would have known what the answer was, would have said that he'd never be anyone's father, never take that risk. He'd known that for years. He could never risk failing a child the way he'd failed his sister Shannon.

But lately he'd started to think that maybe twenty years was long enough to punish himself. Maybe, just maybe, one disastrous mistake didn't have to mean spending a lifetime without a home and family.

But Danny didn't need five minutes of psychoanalytic garbage. He needed a simple answer, as close to the truth as Gage could offer.

"Your mom and I aren't planning on getting married," he said, choosing his words carefully.

"So you're not going to be my dad?" There was no mistaking the disappointment in Danny's voice.

"There aren't any plans in that direction," Gage told him. "But I'll tell you what, if things change, you'll be the first to know. Okay?"

Danny hesitated a moment and then nodded. "Okay." It might not have been the answer he'd been hoping for, but as long as his small world was still intact, he wasn't going to get upset about things he only half understood.

Gage stood before reaching out to ruffle Danny's hair. "See you in the morning."

"Good night, Uncle Gage." Danny slid his legs under the covers and lay back against the pillows.

"Good night, kiddo."

Gage turned away from the bed and found himself face-to-face with Kelsey.

From her expression, it was clear that she'd heard enough of his conversation with Danny to be upset. He caught only a glimpse of eyes before she moved past him, but it was enough for him to see the glitter of tears. He hesitated a moment before continuing on his way out of the room, leaving her alone with Danny.

* * *

When Kelsey left Danny's room, she knew just where to find Gage. Even without the scent of brewing coffee to guide her, she'd known that Gage would be in the kitchen. It was funny how so many of the most important conversations in her life seemed to take place in the kitchen, she thought as she eased her son's bedroom door almost shut. There was probably some profound reason for that, something to do with the kitchen being the heart of the home or some deeprooted tendency to see food as a source of comfort during a crisis. Or maybe it was as simple as the fact that the coffeemaker was in the kitchen.

Not that she gave a damn *why* so many of life's most important moments occurred in the kitchen, she thought. It was just that it gave her something to think about other than wondering what she was going to say to Gage. Or worse, what he was going to say to her. As it happened, his first word was innocuous enough.

"Decaf," he said as she stepped into the kitchen. He barely glanced at her before going to the cupboard and getting out a pair of cups. She noticed that he was favoring his injured leg, his limp more pronounced than it had been for the past couple of days.

"You're spending too much time on that leg," she said. "Let me get the coffee."

"I'm okay," he said, then caught her eye. Though she would never have believed it possible, they were suddenly smiling at each other. "You get the coffee," he conceded. Waving his hand in the direction of the machine, he limped to the table and sat down, stretching his leg out in front of him.

"Is it healing all right?" Kelsey asked as she poured coffee into the cups and carried it to the table. "Should you see a doctor?"

"It's fine." He caught her skeptical look and grinned ruefully. "Really. It just aches a little in the evenings."

"That wouldn't be because you overdo it during the day, would it?"

"Nah."

She shook her head as she sat down across from him and reached for the sugar bowl. "You're as stubborn as Danny."

Just that quickly, the air was full of tension. The mention of Danny had effectively banished the calm facade. There was a long moment of silence, broken only by the clink of Kelsey's spoon against the side of her cup as she stirred sugar into her coffee.

"I won't have Danny hurt," she said, as if continuing a conversation they were already having.

"I agree. Danny's happiness is important to me, too."

"I think you should move out." She hadn't planned on saying it, not now, anyway. Looking at Gage, she saw the impact of the words in the way his jaw tightened, his eyes going blank for a moment as if with shock.

"Why?"

"I think it's best," she said, keeping her voice level with an effort. She wanted to shout at him that it was obvious why he had to move out. He'd been right all along; they couldn't go back to the way things had been. He couldn't even begin to guess just how impossible going back really was.

"If it's about this afternoon, I don't think he was overly traumatized by seeing us kiss," Gage said slowly.

"Of course it's about this afternoon," she snapped. She dropped her spoon on the table with a sharp clank. "Maybe you're right. Maybe seeing us kiss isn't such a big deal. But it brought up questions in his mind. And if he sees us kiss again, it's going to bring up more questions."

"So you figure, if I move out, you're not going to have to deal with those questions." Gage's tone was careful and so reasonable that Kelsey wanted to hit him. "Maybe it will solve the problem for now, but what about in the future?"

"I'm not worried about the future." Not when the present was already so ridiculously complicated.

She stood, pacing across the kitchen to stare out the window over the sink. She could see the arch of the greenhouse outlined against the night sky. She'd been so excited about seeing it finally in place, getting up at three in the morning just to savor the reality of it. She felt a momentary hatred of it, remembering how that evening had ended, thinking how complicated her life had become because of it. If she hadn't bought the damned greenhouse . . .

But that was stupid. She hadn't slept with Gage because of the greenhouse. She'd slept with him because she wanted to. Still did, God help her.

"I'll deal with the future when it happens," she said, turning to look at him. "Right now I'm only concerned with the present and I think it would be easier for all of us if you moved out. Obviously you can still see Danny, but I don't think it's a good idea for the two of us to be living in the same house."

Gage said nothing for a long while. He sat with his hands cupped around his coffee mug, his blue eyes searching as they looked at her. Kelsey did her best to maintain a calm facade beneath that look but she could feel herself starting to crack into a hundred different pieces.

"Running isn't going to change anything, Kelsey," he said just when she was sure the silence was going to go on forever. "I'll move out if that's what you want. But I don't think it's going to make it any easier on you or on Danny. There's something between us. I don't know what it is yet but I don't think it's going to do any good to pretend it doesn't exist."

Kelsey stared at him. He was right, of course. There was something between them, something real and vital that she hadn't been able to ignore or forget. Damn him for making her face it. But there was more weariness than anger in the thought. Because even without this...whatever it was between them, there was still one unbreakable tie. One he didn't even know about yet.

It suddenly struck her as hilariously funny that Gage was trying to make her see the bonds between them when he didn't even know just how powerful those bonds were. She laughed abruptly, the sound holding more than a hint of tears.

"Kelsey?" Gage rose and started toward her, his eyes full of concern.

"I'm okay." She waved one hand to hold him off and drew a deep breath, fighting the urge to just keep laughing, knowing she wasn't that far from complete hysteria. "Sorry. It just struck me as funny."

"What did?" He eyed her uneasily, and Kelsey couldn't suppress a weak giggle.

"You telling me that there are ties between us. You don't even know the half of it."

"I don't?"

"I was going to tell you anyway but not until after you'd moved out." She sighed. "I don't know why I thought you should move out first. It isn't like it's going to change anything. Whether you're here or not, the rabbit still died. Not that they actually use a rabbit anymore." She frowned. "At least I hope they don't use a rabbit."

"What rabbit?" He took hold of her shoulders, his grip a little too tight.

Kelsey looked up at him, feeling utterly calm. She'd been dreading this for weeks, but now that the moment was here, she felt almost detached from what was happening. Poor Gage. At least she'd had time to deal with it.

"What rabbit, Kelsey? Tell me."

"I'm pregnant. I'm going to have your baby."

Chapter 14

Gage couldn't have released Kelsey faster if she'd suddenly burst into flame. He took a quick step back, his eyes locked on her face.

"You can't be," he said hoarsely.

"I am." Now that the words were out, Kelsey felt an enormous sense of relief. It was done. No more secrets, no more lies. "The baby is due in late February."

"We used birth control," he said, as if that proved that she had to be wrong.

"The only birth control that's one hundred percent effective is abstinence," she pointed out dryly.

"I ... God, I don't know...." He thrust his fingers through his hair. His eyes had the dazed look of someone in shock. "I never thought of this."

"Neither did I, but the symptoms are unmistakable."

"You're sure?"

"My doctor confirmed it."

"My God." He ran his fingers through his hair again. His face was pale. He shook his head, his eyes suddenly focusing on her. "Are you all right? What does the doctor say?"

"I'm fine. And the doctor says I'm pregnant."

"Funny," he said without a trace of humor. "You know what I mean."

Obviously this was not the time for witty remarks. Kelsey shrugged, her mouth twisting in a half smile. "Everything is fine. I'm healthy. It looks like a perfectly normal pregnancy."

Normal? That wasn't the word Gage would have used. Incredible, maybe. Unbelievable, definitely. Stunning, absolutely.

"Good." His eyes dropped to her stomach, and he stared at it as if he could see through the fabric of her jeans to the child she carried. "A baby. I can't believe it," he murmured, speaking to himself more than Kelsey.

He felt as if he'd just been kicked in the gut, as if his entire life had just been picked up, thoroughly shaken and then set back down, leaving him to deal with an entirely new world order.

A baby. A baby had never entered into his thinking. He'd just wanted to persuade Kelsey that they couldn't walk away from whatever was between them without taking some time to... Time.

"You must have known for quite a while," he said abruptly. "When did you plan on telling me?"

"I don't know." Kelsey shrugged and moved away from the counter, walking to the table. "I don't think

I had any plans. I'm still getting used to the idea myself."

"I can understand that." Gage couldn't imagine *ever* getting used to the idea.

A baby. *His* baby. His and Kelsey's. He felt a tiny surge of something that could have been excitement. A baby. No matter how many times he repeated it, he couldn't quite make it real.

He was going to be a father. Gage waited for the panic he should have felt at that thought. It was there but it wasn't the overwhelming fear he'd have thought he'd feel. Somewhere over the past few weeks, he'd started to let go of the old fears, started to look to the future rather than the past.

But there was a lot more to consider than how he felt. He limped over to the table and sank into a chair across from Kelsey. She was trailing her finger through a small spill of sugar on the tabletop.

"Do you plan on having the baby?" It was an effort to keep his tone even, revealing nothing of what it cost him to ask that question.

"Are you asking if I've considered abortion?"

"Yes."

"I thought about it." She kept her attention on the aimless movement of her finger, as if the pattern she was creating in the tiny crystals of sugar was of utmost importance. "I can't do it. It's not right for me. I'm sorry if that's what you were hoping would happen but I just can't do it."

"Kelsey." When she didn't look at him, Gage reached across the table and caught her hand in his, holding it until she finally lifted her eyes to his face. "I don't want you to have an abortion. I want this baby."

Saying the words made him realize how true they were. He *did* want this baby, wanted it more than he'd ever wanted anything in his life. Kelsey's eyes searched his, as if weighing his sincerity. Whatever she saw there must have reassured her, because he could feel an easing of the tension in her.

"Me, too," she said quietly. "I want it, too."

"Good." Gage squeezed her hand before releasing it. He sat back in his chair. He longed to know if the fact that it was his child had anything to do with her wanting it, but he decided not to risk asking a question, the answer to which he'd almost certainly not want to hear.

Kelsey was surprised by the relief she felt at having told Gage the truth. No doubt her mother could have quoted some adage about the hazards of keeping secrets or maybe something about weaving tangled webs, but adage or no, it felt as if the weight of the world had been lifted from her. Gage knew. No more hiding. No more pretending. No more worrying that he'd look at her and somehow know the truth.

Besides, now that Gage knew about the baby, she didn't feel so alone. That was something she hadn't expected but maybe she should have. For the past four years, Gage had been the person she'd counted on the most, the one she'd always been able to turn to for help. More often than not, he'd realized what she needed before she did herself.

"Obviously Danny doesn't know," Gage said quietly.

Kelsey felt an abrupt return of her earlier tension. "No." She shook her head. "I don't know what I'm going to say to him, how I'm going to explain it."

"We'll tell him the truth."

"The truth?" Kelsey's laugh held no humor. "That we slept together and now his mother is pregnant by a man other than his father?"

If she'd been less absorbed in her own guilt, Kelsey might have noticed the way Gage flinched back as if her words dealt an actual physical lash. But she wasn't looking at him. Her gaze was turned inward as she wrestled with her own demons.

Gage didn't need psychic powers to know what was on her mind. She was thinking that this should have been Rick's baby, that it should have been Rick sitting here, sharing this joyous piece of news with her. He felt a sudden, fierce resentment of the other man, followed by an immediate surge of guilt. What was wrong with him? Rick had been his best friend. He'd grieved as deeply as anyone when he died. He had to have lost his mind to be resenting him now.

"We'll tell Danny that we made love and now you're going to have a baby," Gage said with a calm he was far from feeling. "He'll accept that, as long as neither one of us makes a big deal out of it."

"I suppose you're right. If we treat this as a normal, everyday event, he probably won't have a problem with it." She laughed abruptly. "I guess having a baby is a normal, everyday event. It just wasn't exactly what I'd had in mind for the next six months."

Kelsey rubbed her fingers across her forehead, and Gage was suddenly aware of her pallor, of the dark smudges under her eyes. He felt a rush of concern. She was obviously exhausted. It wasn't much past nine o'clock, but it hadn't exactly been an uneventful day. And hadn't he heard somewhere that pregnant women were supposed to need more sleep than usual?

"Why don't we call it a day," he said quietly. "You look like a strong wind would blow you right over."

"We haven't settled anything," she said, but it was a weak protest at best. "There are still decisions to make."

"We'll make them tomorrow." He gave her a twisted smile. "I could use a little time to get used to this whole idea anyway."

"I guess there's no rush," she said slowly.

"Nothing that has to be decided in the next eight hours. Why don't you get some rest? And don't worry. Everything is going to work out."

When he said it, she could almost believe it, Kelsey thought. She pushed herself to her feet, suddenly almost sick with exhaustion. Not even ten o'clock, and yet it felt as if this day had already encompassed far more than twenty-four hours. She hesitated, unable to shake the feeling that there should be so much more to be said.

It didn't seem possible that the moment she'd been dreading had come and gone. Gage knew about the baby. There'd been no terrible scene, no fireworks, no explosion of rage or denial. He'd taken the news more calmly than she'd ever imagined. Although now that she thought about it, she wasn't sure just what it was she'd expected him to do. As well as she knew him, why had she expected anything other than what had happened?

She paused in the doorway, turning to look at him. For a moment, she thought his expression was painfully bleak, but it must have been a trick of the light because when he saw her watching him, he immediately smiled. She wanted to say something, to tell him...tell him what? Kelsey didn't even have the words to express the jumble of emotions inside her. She settled for the obvious.

"Good night."

"Good night, Kelsey."

She hesitated a moment longer, caught by the feeling that there was so much more to be said. But she was too tired to think of what it might be. With a slight shake of her head, she left the kitchen, leaving Gage sitting alone at the big table.

Gage hadn't had any particular destination in mind when he began driving. He'd just wanted some time away, time to think. His Corvette, which was stored at his mother's house when he was out of the country, had been sitting in the driveway, courtesy of Cole, who'd brought it over a few days before.

He'd spent the night staring at the ceiling, his mind racing, reeling from the idea that he was going to be a father, to the question of how Kelsey really felt, to what Danny was going to think of the whole situation. He'd fallen asleep somewhere near dawn and awakened a few hours later, feeling as if he hadn't slept at all.

A shower had revived him somewhat, but he'd found himself staring at his own reflection in the mirror, half expecting to see some visible sign of the radical changes that had occurred in his life in the past few hours. There was nothing, of course, unless he counted the dazed look that seemed to linger in his eyes.

He'd wondered what to expect from Kelsey, how she was going to react to seeing him this morning. Now that he knew about the baby, was she going to be any less stiff with him? She had seemed to relax a little last night, but there was no telling how she'd feel after a night's sleep. Weren't pregnant women supposed to be moody and unpredictable? Or was that one of those old wives' tales that were so politically incorrect these days?

As it happened, Gage didn't need to worry about it one way or another. With all that had happened, he'd forgotten that today was Saturday, which meant that Kelsey was at the farmers' market in Santa Barbara, just as she was every Saturday morning. She'd left a note on the kitchen table to remind him.

Gage had crumpled the note in his hand, his expression thoughtful. Was it a good thing that she was going on about business as usual? Did it mean that she was more relaxed about the baby—about him? Or did it just mean that she was glad of an excuse to get out of the house? Shaking his head, he had thrown the note in the trash and poured himself a cup of coffee. With Kelsey at the market and Danny with his grandparents, he had been on his own.

Which was about the time his eyes had fallen on the Vette. Half an hour later, he'd been pulling out of the driveway. The top was off, the wind was in his hair and he could almost believe it was possible to outrun the questions that filled his mind.

With no destination in mind, he simply drove, staying off the highways and sending the low-slung car bumping over country roads for which it was ill suited. It was late afternoon by the time he turned the car and headed for home. He'd left Kelsey a note—about as informative as hers had been—so she wouldn't be concerned, but he was suddenly anxious to see her again.

Since that was the case, Gage was a little surprised to find himself pulling up to the curb in front of his mother's house. But as he pushed open the front door and stepped into the house where he'd spent most of his teenage years, he knew this was exactly where he'd needed to come. Maybe it was even where he'd been headed when he left Kelsey's this morning.

"Mom?" There was no answer, and he wandered through the house looking for her. He found her in the backyard, on her knees in her vegetable garden, a box of seedlings and a watering can beside her.

"Has anyone ever mentioned that it's not a good idea to leave the door unlocked," he asked as he pushed open the screen door and stepped into the backyard.

At the sound of his voice, Rachel tilted her head back, looking at him from under the brim of her scruffy straw hat. She didn't seem at all surprised to see him, but then, he couldn't remember her ever showing surprise at much of anything. Rachel Walker took just about everything life handed her in stride.

"Gage. How are you?"

"Practically good as new," he told her, ignoring her critical assessment of his limping stride.

"I guess you must be if you drove the Corvair over here."

"It's a Corvette, Mom," he corrected her, wincing a little. "A Corvair is something else entirely."

"They're all cars," she said, dismissing the differences with a wave of one gloved hand.

"You shouldn't leave the front door unlocked," he said, knowing better than to get into a discussion of the finer points of automotive design.

"Sam tells me that every time he comes up here. I thought it was because he was a police officer and just couldn't help himself." She gave Gage a reproachful look that said she'd expected better from him.

"It's because he's worried about you, Mom." Gage eased himself down onto the scraggly excuse for a lawn that butted up against her vegetable plot. "The world's not a safe place anymore."

"It never was. That's a fantasy held by people of your generation. Besides, it's not like I'm all alone. Hippo is here. No one's likely to argue with him."

Gage cast a doubtful look at the huge dog, who was currently sprawled in the shade of the big eucalyptus that dominated the back of the yard. It was true that his size could be intimidating until you realized that the biggest hazard he presented was if he ran over you in his hurry to get to his food.

"The only way Hippo is going to offer any protection is if a burglar is covered in dog food and gets licked to death."

"I'm not worried," Rachel said serenely, and Gage knew the conversation was effectively over. He could keep talking, but she'd stopped listening.

Mouse, the cat, picked her way daintily across the lawn and presented her head so that Gage could scratch her ears. Both animals had been named by Cole's daughter, Mary.

The scene was so completely peaceful that Gage felt himself relaxing more than he had in a long time. This was why he'd come to see his mother, this sense of peace that always seemed to be wherever she was. She was content with the silence, busy digging a neat row of holes with her trowel. He knew the silence could continue indefinitely without it bothering her in the least.

"Kelsey's pregnant." Gage hadn't realized he was going to say it until he heard the words.

Rachel tilted her head to look up at him. "I take it it's your baby?"

He nodded. "I just found out last night."

"Is she going to have it?" There was nothing in her tone to indicate that she had an opinion one way or another.

"She says she wants it." Gage reached down and plucked a blade of grass from the scraggly lawn. His mother had never been inclined to waste her gardening time on something as boring as a lawn.

"What about you? Do you want this baby?"

"More than I imagined possible," he said softly.

"Well, that makes things a bit easier," Rachel said, nodding her head.

She lifted a seedling from the box beside her and settled it into the hole she'd prepared. A tip of the watering can filled the hole with water. As the water oozed into the soil, she scooped dirt in around the small root ball, settling the tiny plant into its new home before moving on to the next plant.

Gage watched her work, wondering how many times he'd seen her perform the same task. There was something ineffably soothing about the simple rhythm of the job.

"I never planned on being a father," he said suddenly.

"A lot of things happen in life that we don't plan for." She set another seedling in the ground and carefully watered it into place.

"I've always blamed myself for what happened to Shannon," he said.

"I know." Rachel's hands were not quite steady as she set the watering can down. She sat back on her heels and looked at him. "There was nothing you could have done."

"Wasn't there?" Gage shook his head. "I knew it wasn't Seth's weekend to have her with him. We all knew what the visitation rules were."

"You were sixteen years old. He was her father."

"He was a son of a bitch." Gage's voice held the bite of twenty-year-old anger.

"Yes, he was. If there's any blame for what happened, it's mine." She held up her hand, silencing his protest. "I should never have married him."

"You didn't know what he was," Gage protested.

"No, but I knew it was too soon after your father died." Her dark eyes were unfocused as she looked back down the years, seeing mistakes that were so clear now, so impossible to see at the time. "I was lonely and I thought you boys needed a father. And Seth was kind." She sighed and looked down, pressing her fingers around the seedling she'd just planted, as if to settle it deeper in its new home.

"I should have divorced him sooner but I kept thinking it would work out. And then, after the divorce, when Shannon was born, it seemed as if it had all been worthwhile. She was like a gift from heaven. The four of you started smiling again. She made us laugh again, made us a family again. When Seth insisted on visitation rights, I didn't worry because I knew it wouldn't be long before he got bored with being a father and left us alone. And I didn't worry about Shannon growing up without a father because

I knew she'd have the four of you and that you'd do better than most men could."

Rachel lifted her head to look at him, and Gage saw the glint of tears in her dark eyes. "When Seth took her, I thought I was going to die from the pain of losing her," she said slowly. "But I never, not even for a moment, thought you were to blame."

"I think I always knew that, but you didn't have to blame me because I blamed myself. I kept thinking there was something I should have said, something I should have done, that I should have wrestled her away from him physically if I had to. But I let him bully me into letting him take her."

"You were a boy. He was a grown man. And if he was so far lost to sanity that he'd kidnap Shannon, he probably wouldn't have hesitated to hurt you."

"But I might have been able to stop him." That thought had been with him every day of his life for the past twenty years. If he hadn't given in to Seth Hardesty's threatening tone, maybe Shannon would still be with them instead of being God-knew-where.

"You couldn't have." Rachel's tone left no room for doubt. "You didn't do anything wrong and don't you ever think you did. I told you that at the time, but you didn't believe me."

Gage shook his head. "Maybe you're right. I always figured I'd failed Shannon and I never wanted to take that risk again. I decided I wouldn't have kids because I couldn't trust myself to take care of them."

There was a moment of silence, and then he heard Rachel click her tongue with exasperation. "I had no idea I'd raised such an idiot."

"What?" His eyes jerked to her face. He'd been expecting reassurance or sympathy or even, God forbid, confirmation of his feelings. But he hadn't expected to be called an idiot.

"Really, Gage. You're much too old to be using this as an excuse for avoiding commitment."

"I wasn't—"

Rachel wasn't listening. "I knew you were punishing yourself for what had happened to Shannon. I suspected that you still blamed yourself but I had no idea you were holding on to your guilt like it was a security blanket."

"I wasn't," he protested. Seeing the fire in her eyes, he suddenly felt as if he were five years old again and had been caught stealing his brothers' baseball cards.

"Do you know why you haven't settled down and gotten married these past few years?"

"Because I didn't think I should," he said, flinching at how weak the words sounded once he said them out loud.

"Nonsense!" Rachel jabbed her trowel in his direction. "You haven't been thinking about marriage because you've been in love with Kelsey."

"In love with— You've got to be kidding." He stared at her as if she'd lost her mind. "Of course I haven't been in love with Kelsey. She's Rick's wife. Well, not anymore. But she *was* his wife. And he was my best friend."

"What's that got to do with anything?" she demanded. She jabbed the air with the trowel again.

"I can't be in love with my best friend's wife."

"Why not?"

"Because—" He stopped and stared at her, feeling something crack inside him. His chest actually hurt with the pain of realization. My God, she was right.

He'd loved Kelsey for so long he couldn't even remember when it had happened. At the wedding reception, when he'd touched her hand and felt that
spark of awareness leap between them? Or had it been
later, when she'd welcomed him as Rick's friend,
making him a part of their family? Or maybe it had
been that moment when she'd asked him to be Danny's godfather and laid the baby in his arms, offering
him her trust in a way that had touched his deepest
doubts about himself.

"Sweet Jesus." The words were more prayer than
profanity. He stared past Rachel, seeing half a hundred scenes replay on the screen of his memory—Kelsey laughing, Kelsey's eyes soft with tenderness when
she looked at her son, her face twisted with grief as she
cried in his arms after Rick's death, Kelsey's eyes
smoky gray with passion, her arms reaching up to hold
him.

Of course he loved her. How could he not?

"I do love her," he whispered, speaking to himself
as much as to Rachel.

"Really, Gage, I'm starting to think you're not as
bright as you look." Rachel's voice was teasing, but
her cheeks were damp with tears. "You seem to be the
last one to figure it out. Sam's already lost a hundred
dollars to Keefe because he bet you'd ask her to marry
you before you went back to work in July. And this
past week, he bet Cole another hundred that you'd ask
her before the end of the month."

"Was it that obvious?" Gage couldn't believe he'd
been the only one who hadn't realized how he felt
about Kelsey.

"Only to those of us who know you very well," she
said, taking pity on his dazed expression. "If it makes

you feel better, I don't think Kelsey's any brighter than you are.''

Kelsey. It was one thing for him to have realized that he was in love with her. But that didn't mean she felt the same way about him. Or ever would feel that way. She'd loved Rick a great deal.

"I have to go," he said, standing. He limped over to his mother, careful to avoid the newly planted seedlings. "Thanks, Mom."

She stood and put her arms around him, hugging him fiercely tight. "I love you, Gage. Kelsey and Danny and this new baby are all very lucky to have you. Don't you forget it."

"I'll try not to," he promised, brushing a kiss over her cheek. "I love you, too."

At the back door, he turned back for a moment. "I'll lock the front door on my way out," he called. "Keep it that way." She waved her trowel in acknowledgment, but he doubted she'd change her habits.

Chapter 15

Gage drove straight home. Now that he'd realized how he really felt about Kelsey, he was gripped by a driving need to see her. It was ridiculous. It wasn't as if she was going to look any different, but knowing that didn't lessen the strength of his need to see her.

How could he have been so blind? The question ran through his mind again and again. How could he *not* have known? It had been understandable when Rick was alive. She'd been his best friend's wife. If he'd admitted that his feelings for her were anything more than friendship, it would have made it impossible for him to see her—or Rick, for that matter.

But Rick had been dead for four years now. In all that time, why hadn't it occurred to him that his feelings for Kelsey went much deeper than friendship? The kiss they'd exchanged under that ratty bunch of mistletoe should have been a clue. And if that hadn't been enough, what about the night Kelsey had spent in his bed? The night their child had been conceived? How could he have blinded himself to what that was really about?

He'd actually agreed with Kelsey that they should just pretend that night never happened. All he could offer in his own defense was that he had realized the stupidity of that idea. He'd been coming home to tell Kelsey it wouldn't work. But even then, he hadn't seen the whole truth, hadn't realized why he couldn't get her out of his mind. His mother was right—he was an idiot!

Gage pulled into the driveway and shut the engine off with a quick jerk of the key. He might have been blind, deaf and dumb for the past few years but he was wide-awake now, and he knew for the first time in a long time exactly what he wanted. He wanted Kelsey and the family he'd done his damnedest to deny himself. He wanted the white picket fence and the children and the two cars in the garage—the whole damned kit and caboodle.

He slammed the car door behind him and stood for a moment, just looking at the house. This was home. Not because of the hours he'd spent painting it and making repairs. It was home because it was where Kelsey was, Kelsey and Danny and his unborn child.

He had a sudden memory of Rick, standing in front of this same house, his arm around Kelsey, who'd been holding Danny. The baby couldn't have been more than six months old. They'd been arguing about what color to paint the house. Kelsey wanted white with blue trim, and Rick was accusing her of being too traditional. He'd made alternative suggestions, starting with lavender with purple trim and moving on from there, each more ridiculous than the last until they'd all ended up laughing.

Gage felt grief clench tight and hard in his gut. Rick had been his best friend, almost as close to him as his own brothers. There would never be a time when he didn't regret that Rick hadn't lived out the life he should have had, hadn't had the chance to see Danny learn to throw a ball or ride a bike for the first time. If he could have brought Rick back, could have given him that life, he'd have done it, even knowing how he felt about Kelsey. But nothing could bring Rick back, and life kept moving and you either moved with it or you stopped living. He had no intention of doing that or of letting Kelsey do it, either.

Something, he didn't know what, was telling him that he and Kelsey were meant to be together. Maybe it was pure wishful thinking, but he was going to give it his best shot to make it happen. He didn't think Rick would have begrudged him that.

"I'll take good care of her and Danny," he promised that half-seen ghost. "I'm not trying to take your place. I just want to make one of my own. I think you'd understand that."

He waited, half expecting lightning to strike or thunder to boom over his head. Some sign that he'd been heard, a celestial acknowledgment of his words. But there was nothing. Only this internal feeling of rightness. Maybe that was sign enough. Shaking his head at his own fanciful notions, Gage continued up to the house.

He had no idea what he was going to say to Kelsey. He could hardly walk up to her and tell her he'd finally figured out that he'd been in love with her for years. Just because he'd been struck by this flash of self-knowledge didn't mean the same thing had happened to Kelsey. Hell, for all he knew, she really didn't love him, had never loved him and *would* never love him.

Unlocking the front door, he pushed it open and stepped into the entryway. He was as nervous as a kid on his first date, he realized as he shut the door. Ridiculous. Unless you counted the fact that he felt as if he'd been turned upside down and inside out, nothing had really changed. He had to act naturally with Kelsey.

Unfortunately Kelsey didn't seem to be around. Gage checked the living room, then the kitchen. When she wasn't in either of those places, he wandered out to the gardens. He didn't find Kelsey but, since it was nearly twilight, he really hadn't expected to. He came back to the house and glanced out the front window to confirm what he thought he'd remembered. Her car was in the driveway, but there was no sign of either her or Danny. Danny was probably with Rick's parents. Every few weeks, he spent the weekend with them. This must be one of those weekends.

But that didn't explain Kelsey's absence. Unless she was lying down? Or maybe she'd been taking a shower and slipped in the bathtub. Didn't pregnant women faint sometimes?

Even as he was telling himself that he was behaving like an idiot, Gage was striding toward Kelsey's bedroom. He'd just check to make sure she wasn't lying in a heap on the floor or in the bathroom. She'd probably just gone for a walk. He'd give it at least another fifteen minutes before he began combing the roads for unconscious pregnant women.

But that turned out to be unnecessary. He'd just lifted his hand to knock on Kelsey's bedroom door when he heard a sound from behind it. Obviously she was in there. Equally obvious was the fact that she was crying as if her heart were broken.

Kelsey didn't realize that she was no longer alone until she felt Gage's hands close around her upper arms.

"Go away," she told him, burying her face deeper in the pillow.

"Come here." He ignored her halfhearted protests and lifted her, turning her into his arms as easily as if she were a child.

"Go away," she muttered again, but since her fingers were wound into his shirtfront, Gage quite sensibly ignored her.

"What happened?" He brushed her hair back from her forehead with exquisitely gentle fingers.

Kelsey was beyond answering. All she could do was curl into his strength and sob. She'd thought she needed to be alone to cry out her confusion and her hurt, but now that Gage was holding her, she realized that this was what she needed. He was always there for her. Always.

He let her cry for a little while and then drew back a bit. "You're going to make yourself sick," he told her. "Stop crying and tell me what's wrong? Is Danny all right?"

"Y-yes. Your...mother called," she got out between sobs.

"I just left her. Has something happened? Is she all right?"

"She's fine." Kelsey struggled to get control of herself, gulping back her tears. "She wanted to invite me to a birthday party this next weekend."

"Sam's birthday party?" Gage drew back far enough to look at her. "You're crying because she invited you to Sam's birthday party? You don't have to go if you don't want to."

She gave a short, choked laugh. "It's not that."

"Then what is it? You like Sam, don't you?"

"Of course I do!"

"Mom bakes a mean birthday cake. And she's never had anyone die of ptomaine poisoning. Yet."

"Stop it!" she ordered, torn between laughter and tears. "I'm not worried about the stupid cake."

"Then I don't see what the problem is."

He stretched out one arm and snagged a box of tissues from her dresser. Grateful, Kelsey plucked a handful from the box and blew her nose.

How could she possibly expect him to understand how she felt when she didn't understand it herself. There'd been something in Rachel's voice, a warmth, a sense of understanding. Kelsey couldn't put her finger on exactly what it was, but it had made her feel . . . loved, as if she'd just been made a part of that big, loving family she'd always wanted when she was little.

"What did Mom say that made you cry?" Gage asked. He reached up to brush a lock of hair back from her forehead, and the gentle touch of his fingers was enough to make Kelsey tear up again.

"She asked Danny and me to the party, and I said that I didn't think we should because it was really for family. And she said . . . she said that we *were* family now." Her voice rose to a squeak on the last word as she struggled to hold back another sob. "And I knew it was because you'd told her about the . . . baby, but for a minute I really felt like she meant it." She buried her nose in the tissues, her shoulders heaving with tears.

Gage stared at her, at a loss as to the best way to deal with her. Obviously she was upset. What wasn't so obvious was just what it was that had upset her. She didn't seem to object to his mother's knowing about the baby. In fact, she didn't seem to object to anything Rachel had said. If he understood what was happening, she was actually crying because his mother had been nice to her.

"She *did* mean it," he assured her. "Don't forget this is her grandchild you're carrying." When that only made her cry harder, he decided to try a different tack.

"But don't feel too flattered. Mom will invite almost anyone to join the family. She once brought home the busboy at a restaurant where she'd had dinner and announced that she was adopting him. It took us weeks to get the poor kid back to his family. And there was the old man she stole in the park. He didn't speak any English, which made it really tough. We finally found out that he was visiting from Lithuania and had been trying to ask Mom what time it was when she hustled him into her car and drove off with him. It took ages to find someone who spoke Lithuanian. And all that time spent dealing with the embassy . . ." He shook his head.

Kelsey's laughter was weak, but at least she'd stopped crying. Gage extended the box of tissues again, and she plucked another handful free. She blew her nose and leaned back against his arm, trusting him to support her. She stared at him through swollen eyelids.

"I don't believe you."

"Would I lie to you about my mother's eccentricities?" He put his hand over his heart and tried to look solemn.

"Oh, I believe she kidnapped the busboy and that old man but I don't believe there is a Lithuanian embassy." She gave him a grin that shook a little around the edges, but at least it was a grin.

Gage gave her a crooked smile as he pulled a tissue from the box and began drying her cheeks. "I'll have to talk to Mom, make sure she never upsets you like this again. If it was the idea of seeing my brothers again, I can hardly blame you for crying. I've been known to shed bitter tears at the thought of them."

Kelsey closed her eyes, letting his words roll over her, savoring the feeling of being cared for, of being protected. It wasn't that she couldn't take care of herself. She thought she'd proved that these past few years. But when Gage was around, she knew she didn't *have* to do it alone.

She felt tears start to her eyes again and forced them back with sheer willpower. There was no way for her to explain why his mother's call had upset her so. How could she tell him that hearing his mother say that she was a part of the family had made her realize how desperately she wanted it to be true. Not just because she was carrying Rachel's grandchild, not just because the Walkers seemed to have endlessly open hearts. She wanted to be part of the family the way Sam's wife, Nikki, was—because she was loved.

She wanted Gage to look at her the way his brother looked at his wife—as if his whole world was in her hands.

She wanted him to love her.

Kelsey kept her eyes closed as Gage shifted, settling her more solidly into his arms. Why had it taken her so long to realize that this was where she was meant to be? How could she have been so blind? Why else would she have slept with him? And when she'd found out she was carrying Gage's child, her first reaction had been elation. It was only later that she'd started to think about Rick, to wonder if her excitement over this baby wasn't somehow a betrayal of him.

"Has the baby moved yet?"

At Gage's soft question, Kelsey opened her eyes. He was staring at her stomach as if looking for some evidence that his son or daughter was nestled inside her.

"Not yet. It will be a few weeks before she'll move."

"She?" His eyes shot to hers, brilliant blue and questioning. "Do you know it's a girl?"

"No." Kelsey shrugged self-consciously. "It's just a feeling I have. I always wanted a daughter."

"A little girl," he said quietly. "Yeah, that would be nice."

He touched his fingertips to her stomach, and Kelsey felt the feather-light touch move through her body. She wrapped her fingers around his and pressed his palm to her.

"If it's a girl, we could name her Shannon if you'd like. After your sister."

Gage's head jerked up and he looked at her, his eyes shocked. "How do you know about Shannon?"

"Rick told me," Kelsey said, surprised by his hard tone. "He told me not long after we were married."

"What did he tell you?" he demanded fiercely.

"That Shannon was your half sister, and that you'd been looking after her when her father kidnapped her," she said slowly.

"You knew what happened and you still wanted me to be Danny's godfather?"

"Of course." She gave him a bewildered look. "Rick and I talked about it and we agreed that there was no one else we'd trust."

Gage gave a choked laugh and shook his head. "I don't believe it," he said, seemingly to himself.

"Why not? Obviously we made a good choice. You've always been there for Danny. And for me."

Gage just shook his head and laughed again. They sat without speaking for a little while, Kelsey cradled close in his arms, Gage's hand splayed across her abdomen.

"Marry me."

The words were so quietly spoken that it took Kelsey a moment to grasp what he'd said.

"What?" Her voice rose on a squeak.

"Marry me," he said again.

"I . . . you . . . why?" As soon as the word was out, Kelsey longed to call it back. She was afraid of the answer, afraid he was going to tell her he wanted to marry her because it was practical, because it was the right thing to do.

"I was going to give you a whole list of reasons," Gage said, his eyes still on her stomach. "I was going to tell you it was the sensible thing to do, that it would make things easier. I was even going to drag Danny into it and tell you it would make things simpler for him to understand." He lifted his gaze to her face and

Kelsey felt her heart stop. There was no mistaking what was in his eyes.

"But you're not going to tell me that now?" she whispered, feeling her pulse start to pound. *Please, please, don't let me be imagining it. Let that look mean what I think it means. Please.*

He brought his hand up to touch her face, and Kelsey felt her heart turn over when she felt his fingers tremble.

"I love you," he said softly. "I've loved you for a long time but I was too stupid to realize it." He gave a short, choked laugh. "My mother had to point it out to me. I know there's a lot of things to work out."

"There are?" Kelsey wondered if it was possible to faint from sheer happiness.

"I know you loved Rick," he said, the words difficult to get out. "But I know he wouldn't want you to spend the rest of your life mourning him."

"My mother said the same thing."

"She did?" He blinked at her, thrown off-balance by her comment. He drew a deep breath and continued. "Well, she's right. Rick was never one to hold on to the past."

"No, he wasn't." Kelsey brought her fingers up and brushed a heavy lock of dark hair back from his forehead. "Rick thought the past was a waste of time."

"And he'd be the first to urge you to get on with your life," Gage continued.

"The very first." She traced the thick arcs of his eyebrows with one fingertip.

"I want you to understand that if you don't want to get married, I'll still be here for you and Danny and the baby."

"I've always been able to depend on you," she murmured.

"You don't have to give me an answer now," he replied.

"Yes."

"You can take all the time you want, but I think we could—"

Kelsey pressed her fingers to his mouth, stopping him. "I said yes, Gage."

He caught her hand, dragging it away from his mouth, his grip painfully tight. "Yes?" he asked hoarsely.

"Do you want to know why?" She blinked back tears, focusing on his face.

"Why?"

"Because I love you. When I was talking to your mother, I realized that I've been clinging to the past, holding Rick's ghost up like a shield between me and life, afraid of being hurt again. I'm still afraid of losing you but I'm more afraid of being without you now."

The last word was muffled as his mouth came down on hers. It was a kiss that held passion and promise, tenderness and hope. When it ended, Gage leaned his forehead against Kelsey's and put his hand over her stomach.

"If it's a girl, I don't want to name her Shannon because there's already a Shannon in the family, even if we don't know where she is. How would you feel about naming her Rachel? Because, if it hadn't been for Mom, it might have taken us weeks to get to this point."

Kelsey laughed and put her hand over his. "Let's hear it for interfering mothers-in-law-to-be."

* * * * *

COMING NEXT MONTH

#649 WHO'S THE BOSS?—Linda Turner
Heartbreakers

Single mom Becca Prescott never imagined that her bid for sheriff of Lordsburg, New Mexico, would ignite a battle of the sexes. But Heartbreaker Riley Whitaker was one man who never gave up without a fight—in love or in war.

#650 THE MIRACLE MAN—Sharon Sala
Romantic Traditions: Stranger on the Shore

Washed ashore after a plane crash, Lane Monday found himself on the receiving end of a most indecent proposal. Antonette Hatfield had saved his life and was now requesting his presence in her *bed*. But what Lane didn't know was that Toni had babies on her mind....

#651 THE RETURN OF EDEN McCALL—Judith Duncan
Wide Open Spaces

Brodie Malone was no stranger to pain. His wrong-side-of-the-tracks roots had once pegged him as an outcast, eventually costing him the love of Eden McCall. Now Eden was back. And though Brodie's head told him to stay far away, his heart had other, more intimate, plans.

#652 A MAN WITHOUT A WIFE—Beverly Bird
Wounded Warriors

Ellen Lonetree only wanted to know if the child she had given up was okay. Then her plans changed when sexy single father Dallas Lazo urged her into his life—and his adopted son's. But Ellen wondered how long this ready-made family would last once Dallas learned her secret.

#653 SO LITTLE TIME—Doreen Roberts
Spellbound

Corie Trenton wasn't a huge believer in trust. One betrayal per lifetime had been more than enough. Then Granger Deene literally stumbled onto her doorstep, looking—and acting—extremely out of place. Soon he was challenging her heart and her mind...even as their love defied time....

#654 TEARS OF THE SHAMAN—Rebecca Daniels

Navaho Benjamin Graywolf held nothing but contempt for white women—and the white press. So teaming with reporter Mallory Wakefield on a missing persons case had all the earmarks of big trouble. Especially when their uneasy partnership exploded into passion....

ROMANTIC TRADITIONS

Romantic Traditions sizzles in July 1995 as Sharon Sala's THE MIRACLE MAN, IM #650, explores the suspenseful—and sensual—"Stranger on the Shore" plot line.

Washed ashore after a plane crash, U.S. Marshal Lane Monday found himself on the receiving end of a most indecent proposal. Antonette Hatfield had saved his life and was now requesting his presence in her *bed*. But what Lane didn't know was that Toni had babies on her mind....

Lauded as "Immensely talented" by *Romantic Times* magazine, Sharon Sala is one author you won't want to miss. So return to the classic plot lines you love with THE MIRACLE MAN, and be sure to look for more Romantic Traditions in future months from some of the genre's best, only in—

INTIMATE MOMENTS®
Silhouette®

SIMRT8

He's Too Hot To Handle...but she can take a little heat.

SILHOUETTE

Summer Sizzlers

This summer don't be left in the cold, join Silhouette for the hottest Summer Sizzlers collection. The perfect summer read, on the beach or while vacationing, Summer Sizzlers features sexy heroes who are "Too Hot To Handle." This collection of three new stories is written by bestselling authors Mary Lynn Baxter, Ann Major and Laura Parker.

Available this July wherever Silhouette books are sold.

If you are looking for more titles by

DALLAS SCHULZE

Don't miss this chance to order additional stories by
one of Silhouette's most popular authors:

Silhouette Intimate Moments®

#07377	THE BABY BARGAIN	$3.25	☐
#07462	THE HELL-RAISER	$3.39	☐
#07500	SECONDHAND HUSBAND	$3.50	☐
#07608	A VERY CONVENIENT MARRIAGE	$3.50 U.S.	☐
		$3.99 CAN.	☐

(limited quantities available on certain titles)

TOTAL AMOUNT	$
POSTAGE & HANDLING	$
($1.00 for one book, 50¢ for each additional)	
APPLICABLE TAXES*	$_____
TOTAL PAYABLE	$_____
(Send check or money order—please do not send cash)	

To order, complete this form and send it, along with a check or money order
for the total above, payable to Silhouette Books, to: **In the U.S.:** 3010 Walden
Avenue, P.O. Box 9077, Buffalo, NY 14269-9077; **In Canada:** P.O. Box 636,
Fort Erie, Ontario, L2A 5X3.

Name:_____

Address:_____ City:_____

State/Prov.:_____ Zip/Postal Code:_____

*New York residents remit applicable sales taxes.
 Canadian residents remit applicable GST and provincial taxes.   SDSBACK3

Silhouette®
™

ANNOUNCING THE

PRIZE SURPRISE SWEEPSTAKES!

This month's prize:

L-A-R-G-E—SCREEN PANASONIC TV!

This month, as a special surprise, we're giving away a fabulous FREE TV!

Imagine how delighted you and your family will be to own this brand-new 31" Panasonic** television! It comes with all the latest high-tech features, like a SuperFlat picture tube for a clear, crisp picture...unified remote control...closed-caption decoder...clock and sleep timer, and much more!

The facing page contains two Entry Coupons (as does every book you received this shipment). Complete and return *all* the entry coupons; **the more times you enter, the better your chances of winning the TV!**

Then keep your fingers crossed, because you'll find out by July 15, 1995 if you're the winner!

Remember: The more times you enter, the better your chances of winning!*

PTV KAL

PRIZE SURPRISE

SWEEPSTAKES

OFFICIAL ENTRY COUPON

This entry must be received by: JUNE 30, 1995
This month's winner will be notified by: JULY 15, 1995

YES, I want to win the Panasonic 31" TV! Please enter me in the drawing and let me know if I've won!

Name_____

Address _____ Apt. _____

City   State/Prov.   Zip/Postal Code

Account #_____

Return entry with invoice in reply envelope.

© 1995 HARLEQUIN ENTERPRISES LTD.

CTV KAL

PRIZE SURPRISE

SWEEPSTAKES

OFFICIAL ENTRY COUPON

This entry must be received by: JUNE 30, 1995
This month's winner will be notified by: JULY 15, 1995

YES, I want to win the Panasonic 31" TV! Please enter me in the drawing and let me know if I've won!

Name_____

Address _____ Apt. _____

City   State/Prov.   Zip/Postal Code

Account #_____

Return entry with invoice in reply envelope.

© 1995 HARLEQUIN ENTERPRISES LTD.

CTV KAL

OFFICIAL RULES

PRIZE SURPRISE SWEEPSTAKES 3448

NO PURCHASE OR OBLIGATION NECESSARY

Three Harlequin Reader Service 1995 shipments will contain respectively, coupons for entry into three different prize drawings, one for a Panasonic 31" wide-screen TV, another for a 5-piece Wedgwood china service for eight and the third for a Sharp ViewCam camcorder. To enter any drawing using an Entry Coupon, simply complete and mail according to directions.

There is no obligation to continue using the Reader Service to enter and be eligible for any prize drawing. You may also enter any drawing by hand printing the words "Prize Surprise," your name and address on a 3"x5" card and the name of the prize you wish that entry to be considered for (i.e., Panasonic wide-screen TV, Wedgwood china or Sharp ViewCam). Send your 3"x5" entries via first-class mail (limit: one per envelope) to: Prize Surprise Sweepstakes 3448, c/o the prize you wish that entry to be considered for, P.O. Box 1315, Buffalo, NY 14269-1315, USA or P.O. Box 610, Fort Erie, Ontario L2A 5X3, Canada.

To be eligible for the Panasonic wide-screen TV, entries must be received by 6/30/95; for the Wedgwood china, 8/30/95; and for the Sharp ViewCam, 10/30/95.

Winners will be determined in random drawings conducted under the supervision of D.L. Blair, Inc., an independent judging organization whose decisions are final, from among all eligible entries received for that drawing. Approximate prize values are as follows: Panasonic wide-screen TV ($1,800); Wedgwood china ($840) and Sharp ViewCam ($2,000). Sweepstakes open to residents of the U.S. (except Puerto Rico) and Canada, 18 years of age or older. Employees and immediate family members of Harlequin Enterprises, Ltd., D.L. Blair, Inc., their affiliates, subsidiaries and all other agencies, entities and persons connected with the use, marketing or conduct of this sweepstakes are not eligible. Odds of winning a prize are dependent upon the number of eligible entries received for that drawing. Prize drawing and winner notification for each drawing will occur no later than 15 days after deadline for entry eligibility for that drawing. Limit: one prize to an individual, family or organization. All applicable laws and regulations apply. Sweepstakes offer void wherever prohibited by law. Any litigation within the province of Quebec respecting the conduct and awarding of the prizes in this sweepstakes must be submitted to the Regies des loteries et Courses du Quebec. In order to win a prize, residents of Canada will be required to correctly answer a time-limited arithmetical skill-testing question. Value of prizes are in U.S. currency.

Winners will be obligated to sign and return an Affidavit of Eligibility within 30 days of notification. In the event of noncompliance within this time period, prize may not be awarded. If any prize or prize notification is returned as undeliverable, that prize will not be awarded. By acceptance of a prize, winner consents to use of his/her name, photograph or other likeness for purposes of advertising, trade and promotion on behalf of Harlequin Enterprises, Ltd., without further compensation, unless prohibited by law.

For the names of prizewinners (available after 12/31/95), send a self-addressed, stamped envelope to: Prize Surprise Sweepstakes 3448 Winners, P.O. Box 4200, Blair, NE 68009.

RPZ KAL